It's HOT and COLD in Miami

It's HOT and COLD in Miami

NICOLE RUBEL

Farrar, Straus and Giroux
New York

For Bonnie

Copyright © 2006 by Nicole Rubel
All rights reserved
Distributed in Canada by Douglas & McIntyre Ltd.
Printed in the United States of America
Designed by Nancy Goldenberg and Irene Metaxatos
First edition, 2006
1 3 5 7 9 10 8 6 4 2

www.fsgkidsbooks.com

Library of Congress Cataloging-in-Publication Data
Rubel, Nicole.
    It's hot and cold in Miami / Nicole Rubel.— 1st ed.
        p. cm.
    Summary: In Miami, fifth-grader Rachel always feels invisible next to her
intelligent twin sister until she learns to appreciate her own special talents.
    ISBN-13: 978-0-374-33611-0
    ISBN-10: 0-374-33611-3
    [1. Self-perception—Fiction.   2. Twins—Fiction.   3. Sisters—Fiction.
4. Family Life—Florida—Fiction.   5. Jews—United States—Fiction.
6. Miami (Fla.)—Fiction.]   I. Title.

PZ7.R828 Its 2006
[Fic]—dc22
                                                                    2005045980

MAY 2 2 2006

Contents

1 Half a Brain 3

2 Good-looking 16

3 Potbelly 28

4 Switcheroo 36

5 Man on a Gold Throne 45

6 Honey Cake 52

7 Granny Fanny 67

8 An Ugly Angel 80

9 Tourists from Up North 88

10 Melted Chocolate 94

11 Rebecca's New Nose 108

12 Catwalk 120

13 Alligators 134

14 Manners .144

15 Christmas 152

16 Temple 166

17 Monkey Land 175

18 I Dream of Honey Cake 184

19 I'm an Artist 190

It's HOT and COLD in Miami

1
Half a Brain

I have a theory.

My identical twin sister—Rebecca—and I share our room, our looks, our clothes, our friends, and I believe we share our brain. But we don't share it equally.

When we were growing inside Mom's stomach, I believe Rebecca stole half my brain and added it to hers. With her larger brain, Miss Einstein planned to win Mom and Dad's love and admiration and be the toast of our school. Her plan is working.

Because I have half the brain I should, I'm almost invisible. It's hard getting noticed when she's so bright and I'm

so dull. She always outshines me. But maybe it's best I stay invisible, because horrible things happen when I come into view.

It's a Monday in late September. I am in Mrs. Bunker's room, my fifth-grade classroom. Rebecca is in a different fifth-grade classroom on the other side of the school. Until this year, we've always had the same teacher. I'm still getting used to the change.

Today we are studying climate. Mrs. Bunker asks, "What do people wear in hot desert climates? Do they wear more clothes than we do, or less?"

I think carefully. We live in Miami, Florida. Miami has a hot, humid climate and our classroom is sizzling. In hot weather, I prefer to wear as few clothes as possible, such as shorts, sleeveless shirts, and flip-flops, like anyone. Of course we aren't allowed to dress this way for school. Today I am wearing a cotton shift with pink and white polka dots, and black Mary Janes with short socks.

I catch a whiff of overheated bologna sandwiches coming from the coat closet in the back of the room. Mrs. Bunker looks warm as she stands in front of us. The dark-purple amoeba-like wet spots under her arms are growing larger on her pale lavender dress. She wears two long gray braids wrapped round and round her head like whirling fan

blades. As she waits for somebody to answer the question, Mrs. Bunker nods her head up and down. Maybe she is trying to cool the class with her fan hair.

I raise my hand.

Mrs. Bunker mops her chin with her handkerchief and says, "Yes, Rachel?" She points in my direction.

"They wear just a few clothes," I say. "They're almost naked because it's so hot."

"NAKED!" cries Mrs. Bunker. "NAKED!" she cries again. "They run around NAKED in hot desert climates! Do you really believe that, Rachel Ringwood?"

I'm so embarrassed I feel like *I* am in a hot desert climate. Sweat drips from behind my ears and down the back of my neck. It is slowly trickling behind my kneecaps, down my legs, and into my now-soggy socks. They feel squishy inside my patent-leather shoes. I shake my damp head. If only I could bury myself in desert sand and vanish.

My classmates Eddie Frist and Tony Tombalo are snickering.

"On the contrary," Mrs. Bunker says sternly, "they're not NAKED! They wear lots and lots of clothes, in layers." She points to her gray whirl of twisting braids and says, "They even cover their heads. They need to protect themselves from the sun, sand, and wind."

My sweaty hands leave a wet spot on my notebook as I write "DUMB" in blue ink across the top. I'll never, ever raise my hand again, I tell myself.

Actually, it is the Tree Boys' fault. *The Tree Boys* is my favorite book. The story doesn't take place in modern times. It's about a Stone Age family living in a tree surrounded by jungle animals. No one in the illustrations matches the furry monkey-people I see in other prehistory books. The Tree Boys have long hair on their heads but not on their bodies.

There's a drawing of the Tree Boys on page 1. They're naked and climbing up a tree to their tree hut. You can't tell whether they're boys or girls since they are partly hidden, especially their private parts. But the story tells you right away that they are boys.

Kip was a tree boy.
Tim was a tree boy, too.
The boys lived in a tree.
They lived in a tall, tall tree.

Baby Bark, their little sister, is crawling around naked on the next page with her rear end showing. The person watching her could be Tree Mom or Tree Dad. All you see is an adult sitting naked from behind. You find out it's Mom, because the line under the drawing says:

Mofa was the mother.
She lived in the tree, too.
Mofa loved her Tree Boys.
She loved her Baby Bark.

On another page we meet naked Tree Dad, who is carrying a club and a large bunch of bananas on the jungle floor.

Van was the father.
Van lived in a tree, too.
He was a brave hunter.
He hunted in the trees.

How could it not be boiling hot where the Tree Boys live? After all, the entire family is naked all the time.

I always wish I could leave 1964 behind and go live in a tree with Kip, Tim, and Baby Bark. They have an amazing tree house. I would still wear clothes—maybe just shorts and T-shirts, no shoes. It would be a blast. Mrs. Bunker wouldn't be there, hanging from a vine, wiping her chin with a handkerchief and asking trick questions. Instead, I

would play in the trees with the boys, and help Van gather bananas for my new family.

I could use a new family. Because mine always lets me down. In the real world, Rebecca is the genius princess at the top of our tree family and I am stuck down on the jungle floor.

After lunch—as if my disaster that morning wasn't bad enough—Mrs. Bunker hands back our first social studies report of the year. I get a D and have to bring the report home for my parents to sign.

When we get home, it turns out that Rebecca also has something to show Mom and Dad: a perfect score on a math quiz. They are thrilled with Rebecca, who always gets straight A's. I bet she'd know what kind of clothes people wear in hot desert climates.

Mom and Dad aren't happy with my report. They scold me and then I hear them grumbling about it in the kitchen. If Mom and Dad have their way, sweet white orange blossoms will pour from the sky to make a crown on Rebecca's genius head. And I will have to stick around with a broom to sweep up the mess afterward.

"Time for dinner, girls," yells Mom.

As we settle down at the table, Dad looks at Rebecca and says, "Rachel, I truly believe you are almost as smart as

your sister. You just need to work harder. I work hard and go to my office every day to put food on the table."

Rebecca smiles at first and then frowns. "I'm not Rachel," she says.

I wave at Dad to look in my direction.

"Sorry, Rebecca," he says. "You know, sometimes I get you girls confused."

Then he turns to me and says, "Rachel, I love you very much, but the truth is that Mom and I think you're lazy."

"She just gets by," Mom mutters from her chair as she serves us burnt-skin chicken, baked potatoes, and creamed spinach, my favorite meal in the world. Mom cooks the chicken under the broiler. The skin's not really burnt, it's just crispy and brown. Too bad she picked the worst day of the year to cook it. My appetite has vanished.

After a few bites, Dad puts down his silverware to continue his lecture. "Do you know how lucky you are? Your mother and I had nothing at your age."

"We had nothing," adds Mom, "but the clothes on our backs!"

"Our parents came here from Europe to give us kids a chance at a new and better life. But we were poor. Sometimes we didn't know where we'd get our next meal. By the time I turned ten, I was already helping my parents take care of the family. Neither of them had proper jobs or spoke English. I worked every day after school and yet I still found the time to study and make straight A's like your sister. Rachel, you have no excuse. You've been given everything! Why aren't you making good grades?"

I want to go where they don't have social studies reports and climate questions and smart twin sisters. I want to move into the jungle with the Tree Boys. If I live with Kip, Tim, and Baby Bark, I will only have to keep away from the wild animals that want to eat me for supper. There won't be any report cards.

I chew a big piece of chicken. I can't swallow. I chew and chew.

"What do you have to say for yourself, young lady?" asks Mom, her sharp blue eyes slicing me into pieces. I imagine little flesh-colored hunks of me are falling to the floor.

"Maybe you shouldn't eat so much," she criticizes. "You have stuffed enough chicken in your mouth to fill a football stadium."

Rebecca nudges me with her elbow. "Say something," she whispers. "Mom and Dad are talking to you."

Mom never lets up about my weight. Not only is Rebecca smarter, but this year I've gotten a little heavier

snacking after school on peanut butter sandwiches, while she has stayed thin eating celery and carrot sticks.

I kick my featherweight sister's ankle under the table.

"Ouch!" she cries.

We glare at each other.

"What's going on, you two?" asks Dad, looking stern and wise behind his owlish glasses.

I say nothing. I can't. The chicken sticks before it goes down.

"I think you should answer your mother," Dad says.

My throat is as dry as that hot desert where people wear many layers of clothes. Maybe I swallowed a mouthful of sand, I think. My eyes burn and water as I suddenly see a mirage on the table in front of me. It is a cold glass of skim milk! I slurp it but it doesn't go down my throat. Instead, I start coughing and a glob of milky chicken spurts from my mouth, across the table.

"Rachel, you're disgusting! Leave the table immediately!" yells Mom.

"Rachel!" says Dad when I don't move. "Do what your mother says!"

I get up and run to our room. It isn't my fault I'm dumb, good for nothing, and a total gross-out. Rebecca the thief snatched half my brain!

Mom and Dad's yelling has made me upset and nervous. I creep onto my bed and lie on my back like a half-squashed cockroach. My feeler arms and legs wave wildly as I reach for the covers. I pull the blankets over my buggy eyes. Then I hold tight to Lion-o, my old stuffed lion.

Later, heavy footsteps pound toward Lion-o and me.

"Rachel," says Dad, sitting down heavily on the edge of the bed. "Come out from under there. Here's a tissue."

I push the covers off and sit up to take the tissue. As I do so, I see the tip of a blue furry slipper in the doorway and know Rebecca is spying from just around the corner. She enjoys it when I get in trouble.

"Rachel," says Dad again, "your mother and I love you. We don't want to hurt your feelings. All we want is for you to work harder and do better. Now, tonight, your mother and I just want you to stay in here and think about that."

I don't know what to say. Dad gives me a big hug and I keep my bug arms and legs limp. As he walks to the bedroom door, I hear Rebecca's slippered feet pitter-pat down the hall so he won't catch her.

As I lie in bed, hungry, I listen to the rest of the family watching TV together down the hall. I should crawl away and disappear like the ants after the exterminator visits. Mom and Dad, left with just their genius child, would rejoice.

I think Rebecca wishes I would disappear, too. She doesn't like being around me as much as she used to. Maybe it has something to do with what happened after I messed up in Miss White's class last year.

We had been studying ancient Egypt. One day Miss White gave the class an oral quiz. She called on me and asked, "Rachel, where did Egyptians bury their pharaohs?"

From her desk next to mine Rebecca raised her eyebrows and gave me the you-should-know-this-one look.

I remembered that the word started with *p*. I remembered that it was a triangle-shaped building sitting on sand. I could see Egyptian servants and priests carrying the dead king's body to this place. His body was mummified and wrapped in white bandages. I saw picture writing on the walls, the kind that had people with their eyes drawn with long wavy lines extending from the corners. The eyes reminded me of Mom's after she put on makeup.

I just couldn't remember the *p* word.

"Pyramids," whispered Rebecca.

"Rebecca!" cried Miss White. "Rachel can think for herself." She gave us both an F on the quiz, and Rebecca didn't talk to me for the rest of the day.

"I'm sorry I got you in trouble," I whispered that night as we climbed into bed.

Rebecca didn't answer for a while and I closed my eyes. Then she said, "I don't want to be in the same class as you next year. I am sick of having to help you out all the time."

Her voice was muffled but I heard her loud and clear. I looked over and couldn't see her, because, as usual, she was buried under about twenty stuffed animals. The one thing that Rebecca isn't good at is sleeping. And that's my fault, too. She's had nightmares ever since I made up a funny story about alligator aliens.

In the story, identical twin alligators from outer space land their spaceship in the Florida Everglades. Until the alligator-alien twins discover Earth, they think they are the only twins in the galaxy. But on Earth they find that they are not unique, which makes them angry. Their mission is to rid the planet of twins. They eat the brains of local Florida gators and turn them into twin-eating robots. They command them to chomp down twins wherever they go . . .

The first night I told her the story, Rebecca said I was weird and she didn't believe a word of it, but that's when she started sleeping with her animal army.

2

Good-looking

I'll miss you girls," says Dad as he drives us to school one day. His company, Florida Novelties, sells funny things to stores: alligator handbags, carved coconut heads, and even maracas from Cuba with hand-painted flamingos. Dad goes on sales trips to all sorts of coastal towns. Mom says people love Dad's stuff in beach shops when they're on vacation.

He and Mom have just shared a long kiss goodbye on the front porch, slobbering over each other like a couple of teenagers. She is always very sad when he's gone.

"I wish you girls could grow up to be as beautiful as your mom," says Dad at a stop sign. "Unfortunately, I don't think either of you inherited her looks. You both have my thin, mousy brown hair and small brown eyes."

Dad doesn't mention we both have buckteeth. A beaver could chew up trees with our chompers.

"Mom married you," I say to my shoes, which are kicking the plastic back of his car seat.

"Yes, Mom did marry me, Rebecca," answers Dad.

"That's Rachel," mutters Rebecca, but he doesn't hear her.

"Sorry, girls, but it's different for men. They're not expected to be good-looking, just presentable. Having Adam for a first name didn't hurt my case for Mom's hand in marriage, since her name is Eve. In the Bible, Adam and Eve gave birth to mankind. In Miami, Adam and Eve gave birth to twin girls!"

Dad laughs at his old joke and ends his beauty talk with advice that I know is meant more for me than for Rebecca. "If you don't have the looks, girls, you gotta have the smarts," he says, tapping his head. "That's the only way you'll catch a man."

We arrive at school and Dad pulls over to the concrete

curb. It seems like every kid is looking in our direction as Dad turns in his seat and, one at a time, we lean up front and give him a hug goodbye.

"Take care of your mother while I'm gone," he says as we are slipping out the door. "You know how she gets."

We nod and I give him a toothy smile, but inside I'm an unhappy beaver.

I've always wanted to grow up and have a double wedding with Rebecca. We would live next to each other in pink Spanish-style houses and drive matching yellow sports cars. But if Dad's right, Rebecca is the only one who will be getting married, because she's the one with all the smarts.

Rebecca is looking my way with her small brown eyes. I know she's feeling sorry for me for being so dumb. She turns her head and runs up the steps to Mr. Garibaldi's classroom. I walk slowly to Mrs. Bunker's room and sit at my desk.

I have a theory.

Dad loves Rebecca more than me because someday he is going to need her brainpower. Mom says Dad gets lost in every city he visits trying to find his way from store to store. Rebecca loves looking at maps. She knows the state capitals backward and forward, and she can give Dad driving directions off the top of her head when we're zipping

around town. Recognizing Rebecca's talent, Dad knows he can count on her to show him the way to beach shops in faraway places.

On our bus ride home Rebecca sits and talks with Georgie Sloan. She's our shared best friend. She was Rebecca's friend first, but I kept hanging around so now she's our best friend. She's cute, with long blond hair and a million freckles.

Rebecca and Georgie are talking and I'm not really listening. They are in Mr. Garibaldi's class together. I'm thinking about Mom. Dad always says Mom looks like an Italian movie star. Every day she wears high heels, a tight dark skirt, large dark sunglasses, and her shirt is always partly open in front. I can usually get a peek of her lacy bra. Her breasts look like they're falling out but somehow they stay put. Maybe they're too big or her bra's too small. I want to tell Dad that I wish Mom looked like normal moms. People don't stare at Georgie's mom, who looks like a grownup version of Georgie. But everyone stares at ours, including the produce man at the grocery store, our dry cleaner, and policemen. The other day a policeman stopped Mom for speeding. He turned bright red when he came up to the car window and saw her. He just stuttered a warning about driving too fast and didn't give her a ticket. Rebecca and I

turned red, too. We find it embarrassing when everyone stares.

We say goodbye to Georgie as the bus stops at our street. We live right on the corner. As usual, we walk up the steps, into the house, and straight to the kitchen. As Rebecca pours herself a glass of orange juice, I hear noise from the garage. I open the kitchen door and holler, "Hi, Blondie!"

Blondie is our maid. She comes to help Mom take care of the house a couple of days a week. She's putting a pile of clothes into the washing machine. Blondie reminds me of an ice-cream sandwich. She has dark chocolate skin and wears a white housecoat. She's as big as a refrigerator and is topped off with a blond curly wig.

Blondie is divorced and likes to date. She always says, "Darlings, I can't keep men away from me!"

I find this confusing because Mom says Blondie's fat and should lose some weight.

I walk into the garage and close the door behind me.

"Blondie, is my mom beautiful?" I ask.

Blondie chuckles and nods. "She surely is. And, like bees to honey, men like to buzz around pretty women, particularly difficult ones." Blondie looks at me and smacks her lips together. "Rachel?"

I nod, letting her know it's me.

"Don't worry, baby, men love all kinds of women," she says. "And one day, a very fine man will love you, too."

How did she know what I was thinking?

I go upstairs to finish my homework because tonight we have to go back to our school with our beautiful mom. Tonight there is a PTA spaghetti dinner, and afterward parents get to visit with the teachers. Since Dad is out of town, Mom is taking us by herself.

Soon it's time to go.

"Come, girls," says Mom as her alligator-skin high heels *tap, tap* toward her car. "We're a little late and I'm looking forward to meeting your teachers."

We roar down the street at the speed of light.

"We're an hour late," whispers Rebecca.

I roll my eyes toward the cream-colored car roof.

She whispers again. "I hope we can sit at the cafeteria tables and eat spaghetti with the other families."

"I don't see Mom sitting on a wooden bench sipping bug juice," I hiss back.

"Maybe this time will be different."

"Sure, Miss Goody Two-shoes," I murmur. "Go ahead and ask her."

We screech to a stop at a red light.

"Mom," asks Rebecca, "can we eat dinner at school tonight with the other families?"

"Ersatz!" replies Mom as the light turns green. Her pointed toe hits the gas and we fly forward. "We'll make sandwiches when we get home. Do you want to swallow white gummy garlic bread and overcooked spaghetti covered with red slop?"

We shake our heads to let Mom know we know better. I believe *ersatz* means something that isn't too good.

"Welcome to planet Earth," I whisper to Rebecca. "I can't wait until you ask Mom to join the PTA."

Mom pulls quickly into a spot marked STAFF ONLY and like a gazelle leaps up the school's steps. "Hurry!" she calls.

As we pass the lunchroom we see some stragglers having dinner, but most parents and students have already made their way to the gymnasium. The overheated gym smells like dirty socks and floor wax. Around the perimeter, each teacher has set up a table. Parents and students stand in line in front of their teacher's table, waiting for a chance to chat. It's noisy from the whirling fans behind the tables. The teachers' hair, if they have any, is blowing around their heads. I watch them grab flying papers and stack them in neat piles that fly away again.

I see Mrs. Bunker mopping her face with her handker-

chief. I'm worried she'll tell Mom that Rachel Ringwood is her worst student.

I bet Mr. Garibaldi, Rebecca's teacher, is going to greet Mom and say, "Your daughter Rebecca is my best student."

Mom chooses to visit Mrs. Bunker's table first. My teacher and Mr. Garibaldi, who is at the next table, stare as Mom jingles and jangles toward them across the shiny floor, her heels clicking. Mom is wearing at least ten bracelets on each arm.

I don't think Mr. Garibaldi and Mrs. Bunker care how they look. Everyone says it's snowing when Mr. Garibaldi walks by, because he has the worst case of dandruff in the history of mankind. And behind his back, a lot of kids call him Mr. Scaribaldi because he has a wooden leg. With each crashing footstep, we imagine he's Dr. Frankenstein's monster.

Kids also say Mrs. Bunker is the oldest teacher at school. Everything about her is ancient. The wrinkles on her cheeks remind me of cobwebs. Her dresses are hand-me-downs from Betsy Ross. Even worse is her stained slip. It drags on the floor behind her when she walks. We watch her pull it up, but it just falls down again a minute later. The edge of it is black from sweeping the floor. Why can't Mrs. Bunker buy a new slip? Does she feel naked without that stupid slip?

She always wears an old pin with a cardinal on it. It's so gross a junk store would throw it out. The bird is missing its feet and most of the red jewels that made up its wings. Red is Mrs. Bunker's favorite color. Her bloodred lipstick is never on her mouth. It travels from her lined lips to her chin.

Rebecca and I are right behind Mom as she reaches the fifth-grade teachers' tables. Is it my imagination or is the room suddenly quiet except for the whirl of fans? No—everyone *has* stopped talking to look at Mom. Eddie Frist's mouth drops open, his chin stained with spaghetti sauce. Tony Tombalo's eyeballs are about to explode out of their sockets.

Mom smiles because she knows everyone's looking. She turns around so everyone can get an eyeful. Since we're right there with her, everyone's getting an eyeful of us, too.

You'd think Mom was naked, like the mother in *The Tree Boys*, the way everyone's staring. I'm not sure if they're staring because she's beautiful or because she's different-looking. Most mothers wear large flowered dresses called muumuus. Mom says these dresses should be called moo-moos because they make women look like fat cows. The muumuu-wearing moms seem happy while my mom's un-happy a lot. I wish Mom wore muumuus.

"Rachel, stand up straight!" yells Mom, tossing down her handbag on the table and taking a seat in front of Mrs. Bunker.

I watch Mrs. Bunker put her handkerchief to her nose. Mom's perfume is extra strong tonight.

"Go away, twins," commands Mom, winking at Mrs. Bunker. "We girls have to talk."

Rebecca and I shuffle outside. Rebecca rubs her nose and says, "I bet Mom's wearing a whole bottle of perfume."

Fifteen minutes later, we hear the jingling and jangling coming toward us. When Mom gets to the steps where we are sitting, she puts on Snow Orange lipstick, smacks her lips together, snaps her purse shut, and says to me, "Rachel, stop daydreaming and listen to your teacher!" She smiles at Rebecca. "Mr. Garibaldi says you're doing great!"

I don't need anybody to tell me I'm not paying attention in Mrs. Bunker's class. She's boring and mean and a lot of the time I find it hard to concentrate on what she's saying. Everyone calls her "Birdbrain Bunker," because she cares more about her birds than her students. She always brings sick birds to school in cardboard boxes and tries to nurse them back to health. "It's the pesticide!" she cries. "They spray poison everywhere!" Sometimes they're only baby birds that fell out of nests. She puts watery food in an eyedropper and feeds drops into their little beaks. We watch her try to save the birds, knowing she will fail. Every bird Mrs. Bunker's brought in has died.

In her class I sketch animals, people, and flowers all over my notebooks. Page after page is filled with drawings.

One night Dad was checking my math homework and turned back a few pages in my notebook. "What are these?" he asked, pointing to my sketches and doodles.

"Nothing," I said.

"Well," said Dad, while he studied a drawing of Mrs. Bunker's hand holding a sick blue jay, "if you're going to draw a person, give them a real hand." He lightly sketched a small and delicate human hand next to my drawing. I watched the blue veins in his hand move as he drew. I reminded myself to add blue veins the next time I drew a hand.

"What kind of bird is that?" he asked.

"Blue jay," I said.

"You're not much of an artist," he said.

3
Potbelly

Once in a while after school, Mom drives us to the university pool for a few hours. Today we stop and pick up Georgie on the way.

"Aren't you adorable?" says Mom to Georgie, who is waiting in front of her house. We're late, as usual. "Your yellow swimsuit looks so pretty with your blond hair."

Georgie smiles and gets in.

I think Baby Bark and the Tree Boys might like where Georgie lives. This is one of Miami's older neighborhoods. Some yards remind me of jungles. Vines hang from trees, blue morning glories twist through fences, and egrets walk through tall grass looking for food.

We arrive at the pool's parking lot and step onto the hot asphalt. The Tree Boys would have to wear swimsuits here because no one goes naked. But I wish I could just swim in my street clothes because when I wear a swimsuit everyone can see too much of my body.

Rebecca doesn't have a potbelly—only me, and you see it when I'm naked or in a swimsuit. My stomach's not that big but Mom won't let me forget it. Today I'm wearing a brand-new white cotton bathing suit. It has a lacy piece of fabric attached to the front that covers my chest and belly. That's why I picked it out. I wish I were brave and pretty enough to wear a bathing suit that shows my stomach. Rebecca and Georgie look comfortable in theirs.

My scratchy white towel is wrapped tightly around my stomach. We don't stop and put our things in the locker room, because Mom says it's dirty and full of germs. Mom heads right to the pool, choosing a beige lounge chair under a big blue umbrella and covering it with one of Dad's best sellers, a gigantic state of Florida beach towel. She removes her sunglasses and squints in the sunshine as she tucks her red hair under a black straw turban. She returns

the sunglasses to her face, and unpacks suntan lotion and magazines from the swimming mermaid beach bag, also one of Dad's. She unties her black terry robe and reveals a black one-piece. She lies down, letting her glittery gold sandals fall to the concrete. Rebecca and Georgie set up in chairs next to Mom's. I throw my towel on the ground and step out of my flip-flops. "Coming in?" I ask casually. Rebecca and Georgie shake their heads and both say, "In a minute."

I walk to the edge of the pool and dip my toe in the water. That's when Mom lets me have it.

"No more Jell-O for you, young lady, until you lose that potbelly!" she yells from behind her big sunglasses. "YOU HEAR ME? JUST LOOKING AT YOU MAKES ME DEPRESSED!"

Everyone and their uncles look up from their chairs and stare at my stomach. They're thinking my stomach's really, really big. Like, as big as a house. As big as the refrigerator I'm not supposed to go into anymore. As big as the Atlantic Ocean! As big as the Sahara desert, where I could wear lots of layers and no one would see me!

A fat woman in a white one-piece bathing suit walks by. She's so sunburned she looks like a giant red lobster sticking out of a roll of toilet paper.

Why did I buy a white bathing suit? I look at the woman

and then down at my swimsuit. I bet I look like one of the whales at Miami's Oceanworld aquarium.

I walk away from Mom to the other side of the pool.

Right when I'm about to jump in, I see a carpet of thick brown fur floating on the water. It's attached to a man's back. I stare and stare. That man is as hairy as a gorilla! All he needs is a club and he could star in my favorite book.

I run back to Rebecca and Georgie. "The hairiest man in Miami is in the pool," I whisper. "You gotta see this!"

"Where?" Georgie asks.

"Follow me," I say, and they both jump up to see. Luckily Mom doesn't notice us, because the lifeguard's discovered her. Lifeguards always want to meet my mom. I hope no one drowns while this one has his back turned to the water.

We walk silently around the pool. The blob of hair is bobbing up and down in the water. The ape man stands up and his hairy back faces us.

Georgie whispers, "It's not possible!"

We gawk and he turns around.

Rebecca hisses, "He has fur growing from his head, chin, and eyebrows. Look, it's all over his chest and his back. His armpits, too!"

"Gross!" I holler, and we run. I turn my head and see him

watching me. Suddenly I get a pang in my potbelly for laughing at him.

"No running!" yells the lifeguard, who stops talking to Mom.

We walk fast. There's no way we're swimming by the hairy guy. We decide we're safe near the diving boards.

"Let's do cannonballs off the high dive," says Georgie.

"I can make the biggest splash," says Rebecca.

"No, I can!" I brag, and flash a toothy smile.

We walk past the low diving board. We join the line for the high dive behind the men's diving team. My face turns as red as that lobster woman's skin because the men are almost naked in their tiny black swimsuits. Most of them are cute and well built because they're swimmers. But they don't even see us because we're so young. They notice only the older girls who go to the university.

We watch them climb the ladder to the high-dive platform. One at a time, they soar gracefully into swan dives. It's getting breezy as the last diver flies away. The white lacy piece attached to my swimsuit lifts in the gentle wind. I yank it down to cover my stomach.

Finally, it's our turn. Georgie goes first off the platform. She walks quickly to the end and jumps. Her blond hair looks shiny in the sunlight. We watch her wrap her arms around her knees as she curls into a cannonball. She hits the water. It's not a big splash.

Rebecca scrambles up and walks to the end of the platform. "It's so high up here!" she cries. "A bird could fly into me."

"Cluck, cluck!" I say. "Chick, chick, chick, chicken!"

"Drop dead!" she hollers as she takes a step off the end and goes into a respectable cannonball.

I watch tiny bubbles break the surface as she swims toward the edge of the pool. Then I climb up the ladder. Far away I see Mom reading a magazine. I can almost touch the clouds. It's even windier up here. My swimsuit top is flopping up and down.

"Hurry!" shouts Rebecca while doing the dog paddle far below.

I hear a loud thump behind me. I turn and see the ape man! He is waiting at the top of the ladder behind me. His bushy eyebrows are crawling across his forehead like a giant caterpillar. His eyes are squinting in the bright sunshine. Is he mad at me? I called him gross. I bet he climbed up here to get me! I quickly turn around and slip off the edge before I'm ready.

"Help!" I squeak. My white lacy top flies up and wraps tightly around my face!

I CAN'T SEE! I CAN'T BREATHE! AND MY STOMACH'S SHOWING!

I bet Mom has put down her magazine to watch. Everyone, including the ape man and the entire diving team, must be staring at my colossal stomach.

I feel it growing bigger. I'm the star attraction at Oceanworld's whale show! Panicked people run screaming out of the stands. Others move their seats farther away so the water doesn't swallow them when the pool empties. It's going to be the biggest, most humongous splash in the world!

WHUMP!

I crash belly-first into the water. I feel zillions of pins pricking me as I swim toward the sunlight. I lift my head out of the water and am surprised to see I didn't empty the pool.

Rebecca and Georgie are getting out to sunbathe. But I stay in the water after that, until Mom is waving at me that it's time to go home. I slip out of the water as close to the beige chairs as possible. I wrap my towel around my waist, shove on my flip-flops, and tear out of there.

"Wait for us!" yell Rebecca and Georgie.

"I'll meet you!" I yell back, and run out to the car.

The hot sun is boiling what's left of my brain. Sweat mixed with chlorine drips into my eyes as I wait in the parking lot for them to come.

4

Switcheroo

It's sizzling in Mrs. Bunker's class again today. Perhaps the cafeteria ladies will serve us as lunch to a neighboring school because by the end of the day we'll be cooked. I think about the cool turquoise water in the university pool. I'm so hot I would happily put on my stupid bathing suit and jump in.

We're supposed to be reading quietly at our desks. Tony and Eddie are giggling as they pretend to pick their noses. I have to get out of here. I ask Mrs. Bunker, who's studying *Birds of the Everglades*, if I can get a drink of water.

"Go ahead, Rachel, but hurry back," she says.

My school is a rambling one-story Spanish-style building with pink walls and a red roof. Hallways run every which way and it's easy to get lost. Outside Mrs. Bunker's classroom is the girls' bathroom. Nearby is a doorway that leads from the hallway out to a big grassy courtyard. Some classrooms, including Rebecca's, are lucky to have windows that look out onto it.

I decide to cut across the courtyard to get to the drinking fountain, which is right near Rebecca's classroom. Maybe she'll see me. I run into the blazing sunshine. On the walkway, a grasshopper leaps up in front of me.

I try to catch it, and as I hop around I remember how last summer Dad asked us to catch grasshoppers in our front yard. Usually we don't have many, but last June we had hundreds.

"Those insects are eating my roses!" growled Dad. "Twins, come outside and get them."

"I want to stay in the air-conditioning," I complained.

"I don't want you girls in the house," grumbled Dad. "Your mom is lying down and she needs some peace."

"I'll help," said Rebecca, giving her best butter-up-Dad smile. She pulled my arm and said, "Come, Rachel," in her most mature voice.

It was hot and sweaty work catching grasshoppers. Af-

ter I filled three empty peanut butter jars, I'd had it and walked into the kitchen. I set my jars on the counter, making sure their lids were firmly in place. Then I poured myself a glass of cold orange juice.

"Gross!" cried Rebecca when she came in. "Why did you bring those things in here? Throw them in the trash where they belong."

"Maybe I won't, Miss Goody-Goody," I said. "Today I'm a mad scientist." I took a sip and poured the rest of my juice into the first jar, after twisting off the lid for just a second like an expert. "I'm going to see how well grasshoppers swim in orange juice."

"That's disgusting," said Rebecca.

I placed the second jar in Mom's big freezer in the garage. My scientific mind wondered how long grasshoppers could live in Antarctica.

"What if Mom finds that jar of frozen grasshoppers?" said Rebecca.

Good point. I hid the grasshoppers behind a frozen turkey and some homemade blintzes from Granny Fanny.

Taking Dad's magnifying glass from his desk, I carried the orange-juice-swimming grasshoppers and the third, untouched jar to the sidewalk. Rebecca followed. I opened the untouched jar for a second and pulled out a grasshopper. I

placed a rock on its wings to hold it down. I held the magnifying glass over it. Just as it started to sizzle Dad saw me.

"What are you doing?" he cried. "I didn't ask you to burn grasshoppers! Just get rid of them." He grabbed my two jars and put them in the trash.

After he left, Rebecca said, "I told you to throw them away. Now Dad's mad and it's your fault."

Chasing a grasshopper through the school courtyard today reminds me of my Antarctica grasshoppers in Mom's big freezer. I'd forgotten all about them. The thought of Mom finding the frozen grasshoppers now makes me nervous. Then I get nervous about spending too much time out of class. I run across the courtyard and through the opposite door to the hallway outside my sister's classroom. Right there is the water fountain, and I drink more than a thirsty camel.

Just as I'm about to head back across the courtyard, I hear Rebecca's teacher, Mr. Garibaldi, shout at me from his classroom doorway.

"Rebecca, did you think I wouldn't see you from the window fooling around in the courtyard? No more bathroom privileges for you today. Now back to your seat."

Up close, Mr. Garibaldi's head is huge. Maybe he's part dinosaur or one of those woolly elephants in *The Tree Boys*.

I jump away from him and run out across the courtyard, back toward Mrs. Bunker's class.

Do I hear Mr. Garibaldi's giant shoes pounding behind me? Do I hear him gruffly say, "Fe, fi, fo, fum"?

I slide safely through the doorway of Mrs. Bunker's class and see . . . Rebecca! My sister is sitting at my desk, looking miserable. Mrs. Bunker is writing something on the blackboard and doesn't see me come in.

I don't know what to do, so I go over to my desk and slide onto Rebecca's lap.

"Why are you here?" I whisper to my sister.

Rebecca frantically tells me that Mrs. Bunker thinks she is me and grabbed her when she was going into the bathroom.

"She said I had asked for permission to get a drink of water, not to go to the bathroom. She wouldn't listen when I tried to explain. She just said, 'Rachel, you bad little girl! You've been out of class for fifteen minutes!'"

Mrs. Bunker now has her arms in the air like outspread wings as she tries to cool off in front of the noisy standing fan next to her desk. Then Mr. Garibaldi thunders through the classroom doorway and nearly crashes into her, knocking over the fan. Mr. Garibaldi steadies himself by grabbing on to Eddie's desk, then rescues the fallen fan.

Mrs. Bunker snatches her handkerchief, dabs her chin, and pulls up her slip. As she tidies her hair, poking her braids in place with bobby pins, she notices us twins.

In a moment both teachers are standing over us. "What's going on here?" shrieks Mrs. Bunker.

Rebecca and I are frozen like the grasshoppers in Mom's freezer.

"Who's in my class?" demands Mr. Garibaldi as he scratches his head. A cloud of dandruff floats through the air.

"I am," says Rebecca as I get up so she can slide out. "I'm Rebecca. You're *my* teacher, Mr. Garibaldi."

Mr. Garibaldi walks heavily away with Rebecca.

Mrs. Bunker pats my shoulder with her sticky hand and tells me to take my seat. "We'll talk later," she says. But she never mentions it again and I figure she is embarrassed about confusing us. Or maybe she is distracted by thoughts of the birds of the Everglades.

But I am still in trouble with Rebecca, who got yelled at by her teacher. On our bus ride home, she says, "You're in big trouble for fooling around and getting me in trouble, and I'm telling on you!"

After the bus drops us off, we walk separately into the house and see Mom with Dad, who is leaving on another business trip.

Red Mangrove

Bromeliad

"I'm taking Dad to the airport," says Mom. "We're late and have to hurry."

"Can I go, too?" asks Rebecca. "I have to tell you some-thing."

"Sorry, Rebecca," says Dad, running to the car. "Mom's feeling blue and we need to talk. I'm only going up north for one day. I'll be back Saturday night."

The car screeches out of the driveway. Rebecca has missed her chance to rat on me. She knows better than to try talking to Mom about it after Dad's left on one of his trips.

5

Man on a Gold Throne

It's a Friday afternoon. I roll my bike out of the garage and ride down the block with a small sketchpad and a pencil in the basket. Dad bought the pad for me so I could practice my drawing. All day at school I had thought about how as soon as I got home I would take my bike out and go find something to draw.

Across the street Joy Albright is sitting under a banyan tree in front of her house with her dog, Prince. Joy's a year older than us and goes to a different school. I don't like her very much, because two years ago Prince gobbled down my guinea pig, Little Star. I had let Little Star out of his cage

one day and was standing by as he happily nibbled the grass in our front yard. But then Prince ran over, snatched Little Star, and ran away. I never saw Little Star again.

Joy said she was sorry, but her apology didn't really count because she also said that Little Star would have been safe if I'd kept him in his cage.

Little Star had a tiny white star on his forehead and big buckteeth like mine. With our choppers we could have been related.

Joy waves. Her blond hair glows in the afternoon sunlight. Joy would be cute but she does creepy things with her eyes when she speaks. She looks up, down, right, and left but never at you.

I ride over and say hi.

"Hi, Rebecca or Rachel. Did you know you're going to hell?" she asks, looking down at her sneakers.

"Rachel," I say. "Hell?"

"The place where people swim in rivers of fire," says Joy.

"I think I know what hell is," I say, "but why am I going there?"

Her eyes travel behind me as she replies. "There's only one Jewish family on our block and it's yours. My Sunday school teacher says only Southern Baptists go to heaven. Sweet angels with wings and trumpets will fly around us chosen ones."

I wouldn't mind if sweet angels floated down right now to carry Joy away.

"Jews are the people who killed Jesus and they'll never get in. I have to be careful, too," says Joy. "God is an old man with white hair who sits on a gold throne watching us all the time. He has a big book and He writes down all the things you do wrong. If He catches me doing enough wrong things, I can go to hell, too."

I pull out my sketchpad and pencil from my bicycle basket. I draw a man with white hair and a long beard wearing a robe. I place him on a throne writing in a big book.

"Does he look like this?" I ask.

"No one knows what He looks like!" says Joy. "He lives up there." I watch her point toward the sky.

I look up into the sky and see the Goodyear blimp. "Is God inside the blimp watching us?" I ask.

"No, dummy," says Joy. "You can't see Him. He's *much* higher up." She stands on tiptoes and points to the sky.

Joy's glance is sliding round and round and making me dizzy.

"He watches us all the time," she repeats.

I squint my eyes. I look up and down. I don't see anything but a blimp and Prince. Prince looks hot. His wet fur is matted and he's drooling on Joy's red sneakers. He growls at me when I make eye contact with him.

"Prince should end up in hell for eating Little Star!" I exclaim, and get on my bike and pedal right back home. I don't feel like going anywhere.

I walk into the kitchen and see my sister doing her homework. "Where's Mom?" I ask.

"She's lying down," Rebecca says without lifting her head from her paper.

I ask Rebecca if I can do my homework at the table, too. She shrugs and actually smiles at me when I sit down with my books. I feel better already.

Two days later, Rebecca and I go to Hebrew school at temple. On Sunday mornings, we have no choice. I've asked Mom and Dad a million times why we have to go to religious school when we never go as a family to Friday night services.

"We want you to learn about your rich Jewish heritage," Dad will say, giving us a look that means "Not another word or I'm going to explode." We know it's important to Dad for us to go.

Our temple is a big white building surrounded by palm trees. You go through two heavy doors and leave the warm air behind because you've entered the Antarctic. We always bring thick, furry sweaters because they use tons of air-conditioning in temple. We're also wearing matching dresses because Mom likes us to dress alike when we go out. This in-

cludes going to visit our grandparents, and even going to restaurants and stores. I think she likes being the mother of twins and dressing us alike because everyone makes a fuss.

Mom drives us to temple. As we say goodbye to her from the sidewalk, she inspects our matching outfits. Then she nods, like it's a job well done, and drives off. As usual, we're late and run to class. There are about twenty kids inside sitting at desks.

Mrs. Cohen, our teacher, wears her curly black hair in a bun. She has shiny rhinestone glasses that hang from a gold chain around her neck.

Today Mrs. Cohen says, "I want to talk about heaven and hell. Some religions believe there is a heaven and a hell. They believe if you live a good life, you'll go to heaven when you die. And they also believe if you lead a bad life, you'll go to hell."

Has Joy been talking to Mrs. Cohen, too?

I raise my hand.

"Rachel?" she asks.

I nod. "Will I go to hell for being Jewish?"

I explain what my neighbor said.

"Judaism teaches us to live good lives and make our heaven on earth," says Mrs. Cohen. "Our temple doesn't believe there is a heaven or a hell."

I'm glad to hear it.

Mom picks us up from temple and drives straight home. After lunch, as I wait for the rest of the family to get ready for our weekly visits with my grandparents, I sit on the front lawn, trying to draw a palm tree leaning gently to one side. My tree looks crooked and bent out of shape. I add a wrecked car. That's better, I think, except my coconuts hang like big brown rocks. I'm wondering how to draw lighter-looking coconuts when a brown furry thing with sharp white teeth bites my sketchbook and grabs it.

"Stop, Prince!" yells Joy, running up and wrestling the pad out of his mouth. She returns it gooey with wet chew marks.

"Rachel?" she asks.

I nod.

"I'm sorry," she says, as she looks to the left and then to the right. "And I wasn't trying to be mean the other day. I was just trying to save you. If you become a Southern Baptist and join our church, you can enter the golden gates of heaven."

"Joy," I say, pausing until she actually looks me in the eye, "my Hebrew school teacher says Jews don't believe there is heaven or hell. But call me if the man on the gold throne visits. I'll come over and meet him, okay?"

6

Honey Cake

Today, like every Sunday after lunch, we will drive to Miami Beach to visit our three grandparents. It's always a day filled with enough food to give anyone a stomachache.

First we will visit Dad's parents, who we just call Grandma and Grandpa. Later we'll visit my mom's mother and sister, Granny Fanny and Aunt Florence.

Sitting in the backseat of the car, I try to forget Joy and her dumb comments. Dad's already in the car with us, yawning as we wait for Mom because she takes longer to get dressed. She finally appears in the driveway, brushing her hair as she walks.

Mom climbs in, throws her brush into her handbag, and says, "Twins, I hope you drank your milk today. Remember, drinking milk gives people strong teeth. Strong, clean teeth are important so you don't end up with false ones like Granny Fanny."

Rebecca whispers in my ear, "Mom drinks so much milk, there should be a straw leading from her bedroom to the milk bottle in the refrigerator."

I whisper back, "Dad should buy Mom a cow."

Rebecca giggles.

I pull out my pad and sketch a cow pushing a shopping cart full of milk bottles. Rebecca watches me draw.

I have a theory.

When Rebecca and I were in Mom's stomach, Mom drank one too many glasses of milk. That's why our teeth are so big and strong and look like they can chop down trees.

"Open your eyes and look at the ocean," says Dad. "How many people in the United States can see such a lovely sight?"

I put my pad away in my purse as we drive over the causeway.

I can't help thinking about the song that starts "Over the river and through the woods to Grandmother's house

we go." Now the song is playing in my head. I picture the people in the song riding a sleigh through snow. There isn't ever any snow on the way to our grandparents, but there is the Atlantic Ocean.

The causeway goes over Biscayne Bay, connecting Miami Beach to the rest of the city. I watch motorboats and sailboats below. The sun is burning bright as I scan the water for sharks. Once, I saw a large stingray, but the only thing I spy today are coconuts floating on choppy waves. I roll down the window and crane my neck to get a better look.

"Close the window!" complains Dad. "You're letting in warm air."

"Sorry," I snap, and quickly roll it shut.

Soon our car stops in front of my grandparents' apartment building.

I wave hello to the turquoise sailfish swimming on the side of their building. It looks real until you get up close. The round turquoise windows on the landing for each floor remind me of floating spaceships. We climb the narrow steps to my grandparents' apartment as fallen royal poinciana flowers squish under my sandals. I fan my hot face with my hand. Grandma and Grandpa are waiting at the top of the stairs. They look shorter this week. I wonder if they have shrunk from the heat pouring into their apartment. They never use their air conditioner.

"There's usually a nice breeze in Miami Beach," says Dad, wiping his forehead with a tissue.

"What breeze?" asks Mom. "I think the breezes blew away."

"I could use some of Grandpa's ginger ale," I say.

"It's going to be a volcano in there," adds Rebecca.

Grandpa claps his hands when we reach the top step. Grandma waves. We hug them one at a time and then traipse through the open doorway. It's warm and dark inside the apartment. The bumpy beige curtains are closed and I hear a small fan whirling in the kitchen. We fall into various chairs and couches that smell like mushrooms.

"Sit up straight, Rachel!" scolds Mom. "Don't slouch. Do you want to be short like Grandma?"

"You mean Grandma was tall once?" I ask, looking over at Grandma.

Grandma says nothing, but her eyes blink behind her thick eyeglasses. Grandma rarely speaks.

"Well, I guess she was always short," says Mom. "But she's become shorter from not standing up straight."

We look and see Grandma hunched over. She's not a hunchback, but almost.

"Stand up, girls!" commands Mom. .

We jump out of our seats.

"Now take a deep breath, and lift your chest high in the air. Watch my chest."

We look at Mom's chest. It's easy to see Mom's chest because her shirt is wide open. Mom never fastens the top three buttons.

"Do you see how my chest is high in the air?" she asks.

We nod.

"You'll look like me if you'd just stand up straight," she says.

Rebecca and I have a good laugh and crash back into our mushroomy seats.

"Very funny, girls," says Mom, taking a seat.

"I'm sizzling," says Dad. "Poppa, why aren't you using the air conditioner?"

Grandpa pretends not to hear. Instead he claps his hands again and exclaims, "Who's taller this week? Twins, stand back-to-back." Grandpa claps his hands until Rebecca and I are again standing. He whirls us around so we're back-to-back. Everyone leans over to watch.

"Rebecca looks taller," says Grandpa.

"That's because she's standing up straight," says Mom.

I stand up straighter.

"Look," says Grandpa, and again claps his hands. "They're just the same!"

"Yes, we know," says Dad to Grandpa. "You check every week. Can't we just sit down and relax?"

Rebecca and I return to our seats.

Everything in this apartment is ancient, including my grandpa and grandma. The light brown carpet is icky. Paint is peeling from the ceiling in the kitchen. The green refrigerator is rusty and noisy. Dad offers to buy new things for my grandparents but they always refuse. "I'm just going to have the stuff brought in," says Dad. "Whether you like it or not."

Grandma rises from her chair and walks slowly into the kitchen. I watch, knowing what she's about to do. She bends over an open drawer and pulls out an old pair of rusty scissors . . . She cuts the white-and-red string on a white cardboard box and lifts up a small brown cake . . . She carefully slices it onto four glass plates (she and Grandpa never have any). Grandma serves each one of us a piece of honey cake along with a fork and a napkin. She carries out one plate at a time, holding an old pink-and-green dish towel in her other hand. There is a watermelon painted on the towel. I wish Grandma were cutting open an icy-cold watermelon. It's boiling in here.

"Where did you buy the honey cake?" asks Mom.

"Butterflake," answers Grandma.

"I thought your bakery was Buttercrust Bakery," says Mom.

"The last place was Buttermilk," says Dad.

"Wasn't it the Buttery Bakery?" says Rebecca.

Who cares? I think to myself. The honey cakes are always dry and tasteless no matter where they come from.

"Last time," replies Grandma. "We change bakeries. This one's better."

"I don't believe it," I whisper to Rebecca.

Grandma's lifelong dream is to discover the best honey cake bakery in Miami Beach. As she settles back down in her chair, she keeps an eye on our plates, watching through thick eyeglasses. Her glasses enlarge her brown eyes, making them look as big and wet as used tea bags. They're edged with red. I don't know if Grandma has itchy eyes and rubs them a lot or if she's been crying. She looks unhappy every time we visit.

Dad says Grandpa and Grandma are from a small village in Eastern Europe. During World War I, Russians overran the village and enlisted Grandpa at the end of a sword into the army. Luckily Grandpa ended up only playing the cornet in a Russian army band and later escaped by dressing up as a woman. When the Russians came and took Grandpa, Grandma ran into the woods to hide with her youngest son. Her village was burned. It was wintertime and the child caught cold and died. Maybe she's still sad her baby died. After the war, when Grandpa came home safe, he never played the cornet again. They came to the United States and raised three sons, and one is my dad.

Grandpa jumps up from his chair and claps his hands. "Anyone like a ginger ale to go with your cake?" he asks. We all say yes.

Grandma watches Grandpa trot back and forth handing out tiny clear glasses of ginger ale, first to Mom and Dad.

I whisper to Rebecca, "I just swallowed a mouthful of the Sahara desert."

"Rachel's thirsty!" yells Rebecca.

"Shut up!" I whisper. "You're going to get me into trouble."

"It's polite to wait to be offered," says Mom.

I nod and rub my sweaty eyebrows.

Grandpa at last hands me a ginger ale. I take a big gulp.

"Rachel," says Mom, "sip your soda like a lady. Don't guzzle."

I nod and take smaller sips.

Grandpa sits back down in his chair.

We're eating the honey cake very slowly. Rebecca is taking tiny bites like she's a proper princess.

"Eating kind of daintylike," I say.

She pinches me.

"Ouch!" I cry.

"Calm down, you two!" says Dad.

We aren't allowed sweets at home except Jell-O. When we eat out, I usually gobble down desserts like a wild starving dog, but the honey cake on my plate should be called desert dessert. It's so dry it crumbles when you cut it with a fork. The crumbs are gritty like the sand where those people live wearing many layers of clothes. I take another gulp of ginger ale.

"It's not too sweet," says Dad.

I don't think Dad is a big fan of sweets. He's always saying "It's not too sweet" like that's a good thing.

Dad's right—it's not too sweet. It's more salty than sweet. Maybe the baker got his salt and sugar mixed up. A lot of old people who live in Miami Beach get confused. It's normal to see them driving the wrong way on one-way streets. I wish Grandma would just try the honey cake and taste how bad it is. Maybe then she would buy us a freezing-cold ice-cream cake for our next visit.

Is Grandma sad because she's on a diet and wants a

piece of honey cake? It's hard to tell if Grandma is thin or fat because she wears large flowered sundresses. Somewhere under that big faded red hibiscus is Grandma.

Does Grandpa like honey cake? He never eats any either. Maybe the Russians fed him honey cake. I must remember to ask Dad about it when we leave the apartment.

Dad frowns at his piece of honey cake. He looks up at Grandma's gigantic wet eyes and swallows down an extra-large hunk. Rebecca, "Miss Goody-Goody," is eating hers. Mom has nibbled only a bit of her honey cake and gets away with it because everyone knows she's always watching her figure.

"Is the honey cake moist?" asks Grandma.

Dad slowly chews and says, "Mom, it's delicious," and he points at his plate with his fork.

Grandma nods and pats her chest with the towel. She looks a little happier. Actually, she looks like she's starting to take root and grow into a hibiscus bush. She's planted her hands on both sides of her huge chair. The fabric cover is light green with the crumply texture of moss. Grandma's red-rimmed flower-petal eyes are gazing at my plate. I take another bite of honey cake. Rebecca shows Grandma her clean plate. The giant hibiscus gives my sister a big smile. With green leafy hands she removes her eyeglasses. I blink

my eyes and see Grandma cleaning her eyeglasses with the edge of her dress. Her eyes aren't so enormous! They look like Dad's eyes. She puts her glasses on and looks at my plate again. I look down, too. A small piece of honey cake has survived. I bolt it down. She smiles and gets up to collect all of our plates and glasses.

From his chair, Grandpa points to my hand and asks, "Where's your ring?"

A long time ago, Grandpa used to make watches and jewelry. He made Rebecca and me special rings so everyone could tell us apart. Rebecca's ring read "REB" and my ring read "RACH." I'm afraid to tell Grandpa it slipped off my finger at the beach this summer. A big wave shook it loose. I dug in the sand under my feet and dove in the water, but the ring was gone. I imagine the high tide carried it out to sea and a whale swallowed it.

I smile and say it's at home.

Rebecca gives me a sly look. She knows what happened. She doesn't squeal but she rubs it in by showing everyone her REB ring.

Grandpa claps his hands, shakes his head as if to say it doesn't matter, and asks, "So who's smarter this week, Rebecca or Rachel?"

Grandpa asks this question every Sunday. Grandma is

smiling as if it's the most interesting question she's ever heard. I feel sick.

"We all know Rebecca's the better student," replies Dad. "We hope Rachel will improve this school year."

The honey cake and ginger ale are tossing up and down in my stomach like the Caesar salads Dad makes in the big wooden salad bowl at home. I excuse myself and go to the bathroom. It's even hotter there. I look into the mirror and see sweat dripping down my forehead. My brown hair is sticking to my face like blobs of wet mud. I bend over the toilet and stare at the rusty water. I wish I could throw up. I can't. I shut the toilet lid and return to my seat on the couch. Dad and Grandpa are talking. I think they might be talking politics. I hear Dad say something about someone running for president. When they talk, the rest of us are quiet. Sometimes Mom or Rebecca adds a word or two and Grandpa frowns. I asked Dad about this and he said, "Grandpa is from the old country, where men talk politics and women listen. You must excuse him and not worry about it."

Instead of listening, I watch Grandma. I blink my eyes and now see a giant wilting hibiscus plant, patting its brow with a towel.

"Turn on the air conditioner!" hollers Dad to Grandma. "It's as hot as an oven in here."

I blink my eyes and Grandma is shaking her head.

"Don't worry about the cost," exclaims Dad. "I'll pay for it! How much could it cost? You have a tiny apartment."

Grandpa claps his hands and gets up from his chair to flip on the air conditioner. Everyone sighs as the air conditioner hums to life.

Once we all cool down, Dad stands up and says, "Well, we have to be going to Granny Fanny's."

We never stay long.

7

Granny Fanny

Stuffed with honey cake, we go visit Granny Fanny, my mom's mother, to have a big Sunday supper. She lives in Miami Beach, too, with Mom's sister, Aunt Florence. Granny Fanny is my bitter/sweet grandmother. I love Granny Fanny when she's sweet. Unfortunately she's bitter a lot.

Dad always says, "Granny Fanny's bitter because her husband left her."

"No man runs away from a wife and three young children during the Depression!" Mom will growl, her blue eyes blazing.

I know the Depression means a long time ago when people all over America had very little or nothing.

During the Depression, Mom says, she picked seashells off the sand. She strung them together and made necklaces to sell to the rich tourists from up north. Her family would have starved if she hadn't done this, she says.

When I walk on the sand in Miami Beach I like to imagine a beautiful little girl with red hair and blue eyes picking up baby conchs and whelks and putting them into a cardboard box. But when I look for seashells I hardly find any. I guess my mom picked them all up.

Mom says it was hard growing up without a father. I always wonder why my grandfather ran away. He looks happy and handsome in old black-and-white photographs. Mom says that he was well known for breaking walnuts with his teeth, that he loved to laugh, and that she has missed him her whole life. Maybe Rebecca and I inherited our teeth from Grandfather. It's hard to know since in the photos he's smiling with his mouth shut.

I'm lucky to have Dad. He goes away on a lot of business trips but he always returns.

When Granny Fanny feels extra bitter she exclaims, "Men are no good!"

"Dad's good!" Rebecca and I say back to her. "He's a man."

"Your dad's proved to be a good man," agrees sweet Granny Fanny. But bitter Granny Fanny adds, "Keep away from the rest of them! They want to take something from you and won't give it back. You understand?"

Rebecca and I have no idea what anyone would want from us. We nod because if we don't, bitter Granny Fanny will start praying for our goodness right on the spot.

We agree and say, "Yes, Granny Fanny, men stink."

We've seen pictures of Granny Fanny when she was young. She was good-looking. I wonder why she didn't marry another man after her husband left. Sweet Granny Fanny is a terrific cook and makes the best cheese blintzes with sour cream and blueberries. She brings us chicken soup with matzo balls when we're sick. Bitter Granny Fanny tells us we're ill because we've had bad thoughts and have been thinking of boys. She loudly prays for us as we sip our soup.

The only boys I think about are Tony and Eddie. I think they are creeps and should be gobbled up by sharks. Most likely, the sharks would get a whiff of the stinkers and swim away quickly.

The drive over from Grandpa and Grandma's house

doesn't take long. We park and walk up the two flights of stairs to the apartment. Rebecca rings the doorbell. Granny Fanny opens the door with a crooked smile. She looks different today. Her lips are like two twisted caterpillars dipped in lipstick.

"Mom!" yells my mom. "Where are your teeth?"

"Oh," says sweet Granny Fanny, "I took my dentures out to clean them, and then I put them down somewhere when the phone rang."

"They couldn't have walked away," says Mom. "You look like an old lady without them."

"I *am* an old lady." Sweet Granny Fanny giggles. "It's only teeth. It's nothing," she says, waving us inside.

I like the loose, fleshy skin hanging from Granny Fanny's upper arms. A few years ago we were sitting at the piano pretending to play. I poked at the fatty part of one of her arms as it swung back and forth. Granny Fanny laughed and laughed. I kept poking until Mom walked by.

"What are you doing to your Granny Fanny, Rachel?"

"We're having fun," said Granny Fanny.

"Just stop it!" said Mom. "Your Granny Fanny is too fat. She knows better and should lose weight. What you're do-ing is disgusting."

Granny Fanny is still waving us along as we walk into

the living room. I give her a hug, and as I do I find a fatty love handle to squeeze. It's our little joke.

Sweet Granny Fanny giggles.

"Stop that, Rachel!" yells Mom, her eyes flashing like warning lights.

"Stop what?" yells Aunt Florence, who's vacuuming. Her thin penciled eyebrows jump up as she looks our way. Aunt Florence doesn't have real eyebrows. Mom says she draws them in because a lot of women used to do that a long time ago.

"Put away the vacuum cleaner, Florence," commands Granny Fanny.

Aunt Florence is older than my mom. I don't know how much older, but I bet she was born during the age of pharaohs. The skin on her face and body is dried up. If she sat on a shelf next to Egyptian mummies, no one would know the difference. Her red hair reminds me of Brillo pads. She's tall and skinny like a giraffe, with blue eyes.

Aunt Florence ignores her mother and keeps vacuuming, squinting at the ivory carpet as she looks for dirt. Now she is furiously pushing the vacuum back and forth under the dining room table, which is set for our feast. The table legs are banged and scratched from past cleanings.

Bitter Granny Fanny screams, "Florence! Put it away! Can't you see we have company?"

"What's going on next door?" asks Dad after Aunt Florence shuts off the vacuum and puts it away.

Outside we couldn't help noticing a new construction site on the property next to Granny Fanny's building. The property is covered with many palm trees. The old pink Spanish-style mansion in the middle of the trees is missing most of its roof. There's a large yellow bulldozer parked next to it.

"They're tearing it down," says Granny Fanny.

"Good riddance!" yells Aunt Florence while she fixes her pineapple-print wraparound skirt. Aunt Florence says "Good riddance" and pulls at her clothes a lot.

"I love those royal palms," says Mom. "They may have floated all the way from Cuba as coconuts. That house was built in the twenties. And those mature palm trees are worth a fortune."

"Well, that's progress," says bitter Granny Fanny. "They're putting up a condominium."

"*Arrivederci*, baby!" yells Aunt Florence.

She says "*Arrivederci*, baby" a lot, too.

"But your ocean view will be blocked," says Dad. "What a shame."

"Adios, amigos!" hollers Aunt Florence. She reties her skirt, then checks her blouse buttons to make sure they're closed. Aunt Florence is all skin and bones, so maybe she's worried her clothes might just slip off her if she's not careful.

"Sit down, sit down!" snaps bitter Granny Fanny, heading to the kitchen. "Let's think good thoughts and have some matzo ball soup."

Granny Fanny's matzo balls are light and soft. She says it's the seltzer and baking soda. In the kitchen she's spooning them into our bowls of chicken soup. I volunteer to serve the first course.

Carefully I carry two bowls at a time from the kitchen to the table. I serve Mom and Aunt Florence first. Then I bring Rebecca a bowl and put one where Granny Fanny will sit.

I run back into the kitchen and ask, "Granny Fanny, could you fill my soup bowl with a million matzo balls?"

"I already did." She smiles and hands me two bowls, one of them jam-packed. "The other one is for your father. Did you know your dad's romantic?"

"Romantic?" I ask even though I know the story she's about to tell.

"Yes, before your dad met your mom his name was

Noah. He fell in love the moment he saw your mom. He heard her name was Eve, so he quickly changed his name to Adam. When they dated, he told your mom they were meant to be together, like Adam and Eve. Your dad was silly to pull such a stunt! And before their wedding day, he legalized his new name."

I look at Dad as I place a bowl of soup in front of him. I don't see the romantic guy who changed his name. I see a balding man with thick glasses frowning at his bowl of soup.

"Where's the soup?" he asks.

Oops. I've handed Dad my bowl.

"Is there a fire sale on matzo balls?" inquires Mom, pointing at my bowl.

I pick it up and put the other bowl in front of Dad.

"You might prefer this one," I say, and sit down. Granny Fanny joins us at the table.

"Rachel," says Mom, "matzo balls are so fattening!"

Mom's just jealous. The matzo balls she makes are as hard as golf balls.

For a while nobody talks as we slurp the delicious soup. When we finish, Aunt Florence and Dad talk more about the development next door. Mom helps Granny Fanny clear the soup bowls and follows her into the kitchen. After some muffled banging, the door swings open and they huff and puff as they carry out a huge platter of potted chicken and meatballs. Granny Fanny should have hired a crane. Dad jumps up and helps them set it on the table with a loud thump. Then Aunt Florence and Rebecca get into the act, running back and forth with string beans and mushrooms, sweet potatoes, a lime-cucumber Jell-O mold, beets, baked apples, half-sour pickles, chopped liver, and crackers.

The meal lasts forever as we stuff ourselves silly. Without her teeth, Granny Fanny can eat only the soft stuff. I wish I could share this meal with Kip, Tim, and Baby Bark. I doubt they've ever seen this much food in their jungle tree house.

Finally, one by one, we rest our forks, and then Aunt Florence grabs our plates and carries them to the kitchen sink. She returns with the vacuum, ready to attack the carpet.

"Florence!" exclaims bitter Granny Fanny. "We haven't had dessert."

Aunt Florence pushes the vacuum cleaner into a corner and grumbles, "Good riddance."

Granny Fanny herself brings out apricot rugalach, brownies, and chocolate cheesecake for dessert. Then coffee for the grownups.

I'm putting a piece of every dessert on my plate.

"That's enough, Rachel!" says Mom. "Do you want that belly to keep growing?"

"Leave her alone," says Granny Fanny. "She looks fine."

"Rachel!" shouts Mom.

I return a brownie and a rugalach and bolt down the chocolate cheesecake. Rebecca rolls her eyes and makes a noise like a hog.

I feel like one. After asking to be excused, I walk over to a couch and plop down onto a pile of small pillows. I pull one out and toss it high into the air. As I lean back to catch the pillow something bites my behind! "Ouch!" I cry. "Something bit me!"

"Everyone calm down!" yells Dad as he runs over. "Stand up!" he commands.

I stand up and Dad pries something sticky from the back of my dress.

"It's Granny Fanny's teeth!" shouts Rebecca.

"Gross!" I cry, looking at the disgusting teeth covered with denture adhesive.

"Does your rear end hurt?" asks Rebecca.

"Not really," I say. "It was only a nibble."

Rebecca grins and shows her teeth.

"Oh, there they are!" says sweet Granny Fanny as she grabs her teeth. "Now I remember. I finished soaking my teeth and was about to put them in. The phone rang and I ran to answer it. I must have dropped them on the sofa as I sat down." She pops them into her mouth.

"Oh, God!" screams Aunt Florence while slapping her painted eyebrows. "That's the limit. I can't take it around here! The old lady's nuts."

"You could have washed them," says Mom.

"First I hear how awful I look without teeth," declares bitter Granny Fanny. "Now you complain when I put them in. So many complainers in this family." She walks into the kitchen, the door swinging behind her.

"Adios!" yells Aunt Florence.

"We're sorry," yells Dad. "Please come back and sit down with us."

But Granny Fanny is only getting more food. "Who wants a chocolate?" she asks, carrying in three boxes.

"Why so much candy?" says Mom.

Mom or Dad asks this question every week. Granny Fanny shakes her head and smiles.

I have a theory.

Granny Fanny's friends have a secret pact. No matter

what the occasion, they bring one another boxes of choco-lates. This way, none of them will ever run out.

I pick a chocolate-covered cherry. I pop it into my mouth. I could be in Joy's heaven.

Rebecca and I kiss Aunt Florence and Granny Fanny goodbye. Granny Fanny is smiling. She looks better with teeth.

We drive home over the causeway. Mom turns her head and reminds us to always drink our milk or we'll end up toothless old ladies, like Granny Fanny. We all laugh.

An Ugly Angel

A few houses away from us lives Angel White. He's not the kind of angel Joy had in mind when she talked about heaven. This Angel should live in a doghouse, since he looks like a fat bulldog with a blond crew cut. He's around sixteen years old, but no one knows for sure, because after flunking so many grades he doesn't tell anybody. He has no mom and a dad no one sees, because he drinks too much and stays in bed all day.

One evening after dinner, Rebecca and I are playing follow-the-leader on our bikes. When Rebecca leads the way onto the sidewalk in front of Angel's house, I hear a

door slam and see Angel running toward us. He grabs Rebecca's bicycle before she can escape. Jamming the front wheel between his fat legs, he leans over and growls in her face, "Listen to me, Jew! I don't want you on my property. In fact, nobody wants dirty Jews around here, period. YA HEAR ME?"

Rebecca starts crying. I watch in fear from a few feet away.

"How do you know we're Jewish?" I say.

"You look Jewish," says Angel. "Jews have big noses!"

"I have big teeth, not a big nose!" I cry.

"Maybe Jews have big teeth, too," says Angel. "Anyway, Joy told me. She said you're the only Jewish family on our block."

That Joy is a bigmouth! I hate her and I hate him, too.

"Go away!" I scream. "You don't own this sidewalk."

Angel's eyes bulge out of their sockets. The short blond hairs on his neck are standing straight in the air like a dog's ruff. "This is the last time I'll let you two live!" he barks. "Next time, watch out!"

We ride home like our pants are on fire and tell Mom and Dad.

"Just ignore stupid boys like that," says Dad, putting down his newspaper for only a second.

"We're scared," exclaims Rebecca.

"He says he's going to hurt us," I whisper.

"He sounds like an anti-Semite," Mom replies, while sipping her evening glass of milk. "He's not the last one you'll meet in life."

"He's an ignoramus!" says Dad from behind his paper. "I had to fight kids like that all the time when I was your age! There were three on every corner waiting for me as I walked to and from school. You twins should just learn to lump it or leave it."

Mom tells us to go get ready for bed.

"Rebecca, why doesn't Dad do something?" I ask as we brush our teeth.

"I don't know," she answers after spitting out a mouthful of toothpaste foam. "I guess Dad thinks it will be easier if we just stay away from Angel."

But I can't. Three days later, I see a way to get him. I am riding my bike in front of our house when I notice Angel working on his car in his driveway. The hood is up and he is leaning way into the engine compartment. Without hesitating, I roll quietly down the sidewalk toward him. I'm right behind him and he still hasn't noticed me. As loud as I can I yell, "BOW WOW!" and start pedaling away fast. But Angel is faster. He explodes from underneath the turquoise

hood of the beat-up car. "I told you I was going to kill you!" he cries. He runs behind my bike and grabs the frame. As my bike wobbles, he manages to push my shoulder hard. I crash to the sidewalk. Angel laughs while I lie there with my bike on top of me. Tears are trying to escape my eyes, but I won't let them.

As I pick myself up, ignoring my scrapes and twisted handlebars, Angel keeps laughing. I push my bike back to our house with his snorts following me the whole way.

Rebecca is inside watching television. Part of me wants to talk to her about what happened, but I can't because it would get me in trouble. She would tell. Instead, I head to the kitchen. I pull out two pieces of rye bread and put them on a plate. I spread mustard on one slice and mayonnaise on the other. I add a piece of Swiss cheese. Then I carry my sandwich into the garage and rest it on the washing machine. I open the freezer door and dig out my jar of grasshoppers. I can see they stopped moving a long time ago because they're stuck together and covered with white frost. Pouring out an icy handful, I place them carefully on the cheese. I walk to the wooden storage closet containing the cleaning supplies. There I find more ingredients. I sprinkle scouring powder on top of the cheese and grasshoppers. I pour dish soap over the powder. While spraying on win-

dow cleaner, I start laughing. My plan is to bring the sandwich out to Angel as an apology. I imagine his face as he
takes the first bite. He'll turn beet-red like Granny Fanny's
borscht. He'll grab his throat and bend over as he throws
up pieces of grasshopper arms and legs. Joy's dog, Prince,
will come sniffing and will eat the poisoned, spit-up grasshoppers. I will stand over both of them and laugh as they
roll around in pain on the sidewalk at my feet.

Blondie pokes her head out the kitchen doorway and
asks, "Girl, what's so funny?"

"I'm making a delicious lunch for that bully, Angel," I
explain. "It's a meal he'll never forget."

"You mean that big nasty blond boy down the street?"
she asks.

I laugh and add another ingredient. Her eyes go wide
when she realizes what I'm doing.

I laugh and laugh until I'm crying.

"Let me help you throw this away," says Blondie. She
carefully picks up my sandwich and carries it to the outside
trash cans. I hear the backs of her slippers slapping the
bottoms of her feet and then the metal clang of the lid as
she opens and shuts the can.

She comes back and leads me inside, straight to the
bathroom. I try to talk but she shushes me.

"Child, don't ever do that again. Those chemicals are dangerous, especially if you mix them."

She closes the door behind us and makes me sit down on the toilet seat lid. She perches on the edge of the bathtub and cleans me up with a cool washcloth. Next she brushes my hair. Then she stands up and asks me to tell her exactly what's going on.

As I talk, she stares at me with her hands firmly in place on her wide, wide hips. There's a film of moisture on Blondie's top lip. I've never seen her so upset, except the time we put roller skates in the dryer.

"Look, honey," Blondie says softly when I finish telling her about Angel. "A lot of people will hate you just for being Jewish. A lot of people hate colored folks like me. You might as well learn to turn the other cheek. There's nothing you can do about it, except learn how to live with it. You don't really want to hurt these people. Just stay out of their way. Get it?"

I nod and she wraps me up in an enormous hug.

"Listen here," calls Blondie as she opens the bathroom door, "never let foolish people make you do foolish things. That poor ignorant boy down the street is heading for big trouble. I won't be surprised if he ends up behind bars one day. If you do something foolish, you could land in jail, and, believe me, jail's not worth it! Now, why don't you stay in here for a little while just to calm down?"

I nod again. The door shuts behind her, and I know I love Blondie even more than I hate Angel.

9
Tourists from Up North

Wish you were here!

It's another Sunday afternoon and again we're walking up the steps to Grandma and Grandpa's.

"It's too hot to sit in that stuffy apartment," says Mom.

"It's a beautiful day. Grandpa and Grandma need fresh air," says Dad. "Let's go for a walk on Lincoln Road after the honey cake."

"Eat quickly, girls. But don't make a spectacle of your-selves," Mom advises.

As Mom and Dad nibble politely, Rebecca and I gobble down our honey cake. I start choking and coughing. A dry chunk is caught in my throat.

"Rachel, goodness, are you all right?" asks Mom.

Grandpa comes out from the kitchen with a frosty glass of ginger ale. I take a small, ladylike sip and the chunk slides toward my stomach.

Soon Rebecca and I march out of the apartment and wait while Grandma and Grandpa carefully inch their way down the stairs, with Mom and Dad behind them. We slowly make our way two blocks to Lincoln Road, a pretty street with lots of stores. Tropical trees and bubbling tiled fountains are planted in the middle. This is one of the only streets in Miami where cars aren't allowed.

"Let's walk in the shade," says Mom, squinting in the bright sunlight. We cross to the cooler side of the street. We don't shop but we do look in every store window. Bit by bit, taking tiny steps, my grandparents shuffle forward. Rebecca and I run ahead, watching for tourists from up north.

Dad always says that tourists like to visit Miami Beach in the fall and winter because it's freezing and miserable up north. Everyone from up there is overjoyed to be in Miami.

Dad's right. They're so happy they lose their minds. Sometimes we watch them swim in the ocean as we walk by bundled in sweaters. The local TV reporters call them "snowbirds."

A short, round man wearing a light yellow cap, a yellow shirt, a yellow belt, yellow shoes, and yellow-and-orange-checked pants walks by with his wife. He's puffing a fat, smelly cigar. As he approaches us, he grumbles loudly to the air, "I'm hot. Where can I get a cold drink?"

His wife wears a pale pink flowered scarf, pink lipstick, a pink shirt, pink heels, and pink pants. "You don't have to yell, Mort!" she says. "Everyone from here to Jersey can hear you!" She lowers her head and looks at us. We can't see her eyes behind her dark sunglasses, but her pink mouth is smiling.

We're smiling, too, because we think they look hilarious.

I have a theory.

People from up north receive Miami postcards from other tourists who visit from up north. The cards show pink flamingos, green alligators, and bright red parrots. They think they'll fit in if they dress in bright colors, too.

"Look, Helen," says the man. "They're twins."

"They look exactly alike," she says. "But someone should speak to their mother about braces for their teeth."

Rebecca and I instantly close our mouths.

The man leans in for a closer look. He almost falls, and he's shaking as he straightens up.

He reminds me of quivering lemon Jell-O.

"Are you girls sure you know which one you are when

you wake up in the morning?" he asks, blowing smoke rings in our faces.

Rebecca answers, "Of course we do," and gives him a big beaver smile.

"Would you happen to know a good place where the natives eat?" he asks.

We stare at him.

"Natives?" I ask. "You mean the ones who live in jungles and swing from trees?"

"The local yokels," says the pink lady. "You know, the people who actually reside here in south Florida."

"Oh, yes," I say. "I know where you can eat alligator-feet sandwiches served with rattlesnake salad and mosquito punch, a south Florida treat!"

Mr. Lemon Jell-O shakes his head and says, "Do all the children around here have such bad manners?"

"Who has bad manners?" asks Mom, walking up with Dad, Grandpa, and Grandma.

The man pokes his cigar in our direction and explains.

"Apologize now!" yells Dad.

"I don't have bad manners!" says Rebecca. "It was all bigmouth Rachel's fault."

"But, Dad," I want to say, "they are the ones who don't have manners." Instead, I keep my big mouth shut.

"You girls should always be polite to your elders," Dad scolds.

"We're sorry," we say together.

Dad gives the couple directions to a nearby restaurant. We watch them smile and walk away.

"I'm raising savages!" cries Mom.

Grandpa claps his hands and says, "Everything's all right. Let's go home. Grandma is tired."

We start walking back on the same shaded side of the street.

"Thanks a lot for getting me in trouble," grumbles Rebecca.

Me and my big mouth. I should cement it shut. I kick at a crack in the sidewalk.

We reach the apartment and kiss Grandma and Grandpa goodbye. In the backseat of the car, Rebecca leans over and whispers in my ear, "I hope Granny Fanny serves alligator-feet sandwiches and mosquito punch. I'm starving."

I smile and take a deep breath. I'm relieved Rebecca isn't really mad at me.

I think about my plan to visit "up north" someday. It's only fair since they're always visiting down here.

10
Melted Chocolate

The threat of ending up toothless like Granny Fanny is Mom and Dad's warning every Halloween. They allow us to trick-or-treat, but upon entering the house we're told to pick out ten pieces of candy to keep. The rest is given to Blondie.

Rebecca and I have just finished putting on our costumes when Mom walks into our room holding a glass of milk.

"For once, can we keep all our candy?" I ask hopefully while standing in front of our closet so she can't see it's a big mess.

"Do you want rotten teeth?" she answers. "Candy's ersatz!"

"Georgie keeps her candy," replies Rebecca. "She has teeth."

"Do you want to be exactly like your little friends?" asks Mom. "If they jumped off a cliff, would you follow?"

Rebecca and I look at each other and shake our heads.

"Aren't you worried about Blondie's teeth?" I ask.

Mom sips her milk and says, "Blondie's an adult and can make up her own mind." She leaves, slamming the door behind her.

I feel invisible. My costume is a beautiful butterfly and Mom didn't notice. I made it myself. I took wire hangers and bent them into the shape of wings. Then I taped brown paper over them and painted them with turquoise, pink, and purple polka dots. I glued yellow feathers around the edges to make them flutter as I walk. Rebecca helped me attach my wings to my T-shirt with safety pins and tape. My antennas are long yellow pipe cleaners pushed into yellow Ping-Pong balls and then bobby-pinned to my hair.

"No one else will have your costume because it isn't store-bought like mine," says Rebecca.

Rebecca's a boring witch from some TV show. She's

wearing a black dress, black cape, black hat, and carries a small broom she borrowed from Blondie. The only neat thing about Rebecca's costume is that she's blackened her teeth. According to Mom, our teeth will look just like Rebecca's if we eat Halloween candy.

We grab brown grocery bags and run out the front door. Mom waves goodbye. When the door closes behind her, I see the lights outside our house turn off. I guess Mom's saving the neighborhood from tooth decay.

"It's starting to sprinkle," says Rebecca. "Should I run and get an umbrella?"

"No way," I say. "Mom might change her mind and not let you back outside. Dad will be home any minute and he'll agree with her."

Rebecca nods. We race down the block and across the street. We take turns ringing the doorbells. "Trick or treat!" we yell.

"What do we have here?" asks a really big man.

The smell of cigarettes and something moldy comes from inside his house.

"Do I see a bug and a witch?" says the man.

"Butterfly," I say nervously, holding out my bag.

"How inventive," he says with a smile.

His rotten teeth look real. I bet there are a million bodies buried under his living room floor.

"We have to go," I yelp, and grab Rebecca's arm.

"Relax, Rachel," says Rebecca as he drops small boxes of candy corn into our bags.

I run to the sidewalk.

"Wait up!" yells Rebecca.

"The bogeyman lives there!" I say. "There's a rotten smell in his house. Did you see his teeth?"

"You're so dramatic, Rachel! He was a nice man with bad teeth," says Rebecca. "Look, isn't that Joy trick-or-treating with her little brother across the street?"

Joy is dressed as Cinderella and looks pretty. She's wearing a layered green gown made from satin and lace fabrics. She's holding up the bottom so it doesn't get muddy. Her long blond hair is tucked under a tall yellow wig that would look great on Blondie. Red sneakers peek out from under her wide skirt instead of glass slippers. Her brother is a pumpkin. His upper body is inside a giant ball made from newspaper and painted orange. His face is painted green and there are fabric leaves twisted around his neck. It's one of the best costumes I've ever seen.

I hope that Joy won't notice us, but she does. Rebecca drags me over.

"Hi, twins," says Joy, staring at a palm tree. "Isn't my brother adorable? My mom made his costume and mine, too."

"Your mom's really talented," I say, wondering what it would be like to have Mom make my costume. "Stand up straight or you'll wreck all my hard work!" I hear her scold. I shake my head.

"Who is what?" asks Joy.

"I'm Rebecca the witch," says Rebecca, showing a blackened smile.

"Then what are you, Rachel?" Joy asks. She squints as she examines my costume.

"A butterfly."

"Really?" asks Joy, like she doesn't believe it.

"Really."

"Are you going to Carla's house?" Joy points across the street.

"Yeah," I say. "Aren't you?"

"No!" Joy says, looking horrified. "Did you know Carla's Italian?"

"So what?" I say.

"They're Catholic," whispers Joy. "You know what else?

My mom says Catholics don't believe in divorce, but Carla's parents got divorced and just remarried!"

"Good grief," I say. "Like that matters. We have to go, Joy."

At Carla's house, I ring the doorbell and Carla appears, dressed as Barbie. No surprise there. She has the best Barbie collection I've ever seen. I like Carla even more because her mom's a little like mine.

"Hi, Carla!" says Rebecca. "Why aren't you trick-or-treating?"

"My parents are having a Halloween party later!" she says. "They're getting ready and want me to give out the candy."

Carla's eyes bounce between my sister and me.

"Rachel the butterfly and Rebecca the witch," she guesses.

"Right!" I say. I can tell Carla's Barbie costume is store-bought. She looks great.

"Close the door!" yells a voice from behind Carla. "You're letting out the air-conditioning! Do you want to cool off all of Miami?" Carla's mom totters toward us on really tall and sparkly high heels. She's wrapped in a white sheet from her chest to just above her knees. Her eyelashes and lips are painted gold. She waves a gold cigarette holder

in our direction and says, "Hellllloooo, children," and carefully walks back down the hallway.

"What's your mom's costume?" asks Rebecca.

"Aphrodite, the Greek goddess of love." Carla giggles. "You should see my dad. He's Zeus. You know, the king of the Greek gods. They're about to have a getting-back-together toast. I have to go!"

She plonks a candy bar into each of our bags and we take off.

Crybaby Stevens runs by. You have to be careful with Crybaby. His real name is Gary, but all you have to do is touch him and he starts crying. We decide to walk in the other direction.

"Oh, no," I say. "It's really raining now. I think one of my butterfly wings is loose. It's bumping up and down as I walk."

"You'll be okay," says Rebecca after checking. "But most of your yellow feathers are gone."

I turn my head and see that the painted polka dots have started to run. We ring another doorbell. "Trick or treat!" we yell.

"How adorable!" cries a small woman holding a foxlike dog. The dog leaps out of her arms and into my candy bag. "Freddy!" cries the woman. She leans over, pulls Freddy out,

and places him on the floor. The woman gives us each two boxes of chocolate-covered raisins. Freddy chews on my sneaker laces and I try to push him away. Suddenly my loose wing snaps and lands on poor Freddy's head.

Freddy yelps.

"My baby!" cries the woman. She grabs Freddy and slams the door. She would probably take back her candy if she could.

I toss the broken wing into her hibiscus hedge. My antennas are falling and hitting me in the face.

"You look icky," says Rebecca.

I wish I'd taken a white sheet, cut two holes in it, thrown it over my head, and been a ghost. Why did I have to be so original anyway? Rebecca looks fine, and I bet that store-bought witch's cape is keeping her dry.

"Oh, gross-me-out-the-door!" exclaims Rebecca. "Here comes Tony Tombalo and Eddie Frist."

"Hey, Rachel and Rebecca Ringworm!" says Eddie.

Eddie's dressed as a jailbird. He's wearing black-and-white-striped pajamas, and a black rubber ball is attached to one of his legs with a chain. Tony's a pirate. He's wearing an eye patch, and a stuffed parrot is attached to his shoulder. Their costumes are terrific, which makes me feel really, really bad.

"Eeeeewwww!" says Tony, pointing at me. "You look like something I threw up when I had the flu. What are you anyway?"

"None of your beeswax, Tony Tombstone and Eddie Fishhead!" I yell.

They laugh and run away.

"It's late," says Rebecca. "We should go home."

I can barely carry my full bag of candy. I have a plan and it's time to put it into action. "You know, Rebecca," I say, "Mom and Dad are going to grab our candy the moment we walk in."

"We're allowed to keep *some* candy," says Rebecca.

"No one can take our candy if we eat it!" I declare, jumping up and down as my other wing rips and falls to the ground. I kick it under a parked car.

Rebecca's smart enough to know a brilliant idea when she hears one. She nods and grabs a chocolate bar.

I stuff a cherry lollipop into one side of my mouth and some bite-size caramels into the other. I chow down vanilla taffy, candy corn, a peanut butter crunch bar, and a whole bunch of other stuff.

"I have to slow down," I say.

"Let's just take one bite out of the good stuff," says Rebecca, laughing.

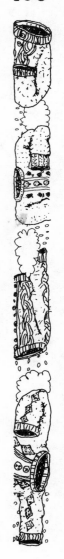

I pull out a roll of Life Savers. I pop one into my mouth and throw the rest over my head. Superman and two ghosts run by, splashing through the puddles. They stop and stare at us as we throw half-eaten candy into the air.

Soon our bags are almost empty except for junk like party mints, black licorice, and raisins.

"Hello, girls," Dad says as we walk inside our house.

I bet he's going to give us a speech on tooth decay.

Instead he surprises us.

"Your mother and I have decided that this year— Ah, Rachel? What in the world were you dressed as tonight?"

I rip the broken antennas off my head and throw them in the trash.

"Nothing," I say.

"Well, anyway," says Dad, "we've decided you can keep your Halloween candy this year. Mom and I think you're old enough to not overdo it."

Rebecca and I stare at him.

"That's not fair!" I scream. "We threw most of it away."

"Then I guess you girls already made the right decision," says Dad, smiling.

Angry tears dribble down my face. I feel so stuffed with sugar that I'm afraid to move because candy might trickle

out my ears or nose. I feel it oozing up my throat. Rebecca is rubbing her stomach.

"Rachel, you and your stupid ideas!" she cries.

My stomach hurts, too. I may have suggested eating all the candy, but Rebecca didn't have to listen to me.

I look up at Dad and plead, "Can we run out and get some more for later?"

"Calm down," he says, shaking his head. "You've had enough fun scampering around the neighborhood. Go brush your teeth and get into bed."

Rebecca burps. She's turning green and now really looks like a witch. She's going to throw up! I grab her arm and yell, "Good night, Dad!"

We race to the bathroom. Rebecca sticks her head in the toilet and unloads like a dump truck. I hold my nose and hand her a towel. We brush the sugar from our teeth, climb into bed, and dream about a world made of candy.

In the morning it's warm and muggy as Rebecca and I track last night's trick-or-treat trail. Colorful blobs of half-bitten candy are melting on the sidewalk.

"Guess what!" hollers Joy from her yard. "Angel's in jail. He was arrested last night for stealing a car!"

"Good," I mutter. "I hope he stays there forever."

We stare at Prince. He's come over and is licking melted candy corn off the sidewalk.

"They're sending him to some kind of place for bad boys," says Joy, and waves goodbye.

Rebecca and I smile. Angel won't be bothering us anymore.

Up ahead, there are tiny pieces of candy moving slowly across the sidewalk. Rebecca points to a long line of ants carrying them away.

11

Rebecca's New Nose

Napoleon   Groucho   Cleopatra

Noses
for
Sale

Mom and Dad are shopping in South Miami for a brand-new house. Today we get to go with them.

"I hope it's yellow," I say. "A yellow house is sunny."

"I hope it has a pool," cries Rebecca.

A smiling saleslady greets us at the door of a "just built" white house.

"Aren't you two cute in your matching blue dresses!" says the lady. "You must be twins."

We smile and watch her stop smiling as she sees our teeth.

"Come on inside," she says quickly.

Rebecca runs into the living room and yells, "I see a swimming pool! We can have swim parties."

"Take it easy," Dad warns. "I want you girls on your best behavior while Mom and I speak with the Realtor."

"Let me show you the bedrooms," says the lady, leading Mom and Dad away.

Rebecca smacks me on the back and squeals, "Tag, you're it!"

I chase her through the light-filled living room, into the kitchen and dining room, back into the living room. I'm just about to catch her when Rebecca decides to head outside to the swimming pool . . . and runs straight into a closed sliding glass door! I stop short and shriek as Rebecca and shards of glass crash to the floor.

"Rebecca!" I cry.

Dad comes running and pushes me out of the way. He carefully picks up my sister, and a million little pieces of glass shower off her dress. Luckily there is a working phone in the house; the saleslady is already calling an ambulance. With Mom right behind them, Dad carries Rebecca to the large white kitchen and sits her on the edge of the sink, where he uses the sprayer to clean the glass off her face and arms. Rebecca's shiny black patent-leather shoes are kicking wildly.

The empty house is filled with the sound of her screams. I stand on my tiptoes and see her baby-blue dress turning bright red. Blood is turning the sink bright red. I can't see her face! Has Rebecca lost her face?

Mom's face is red and angry. The saleslady's face is frozen into a stiff grimace.

"It was an accident!" I cry, wishing I were invisible.

Rebecca's loud cries become soft whimpers. I'm asked to wait in the living room. Soon two men in white arrive with a stretcher and take her away to their ambulance. Mom follows after them, slamming the front door. She'll go with Rebecca to the hospital. I hear her high heels clicking down the sidewalk, then the ambulance doors locking shut.

After the siren fades away, Dad turns to me and gives me a look of anger mixed with disappointment that I'll never forget. Dad offers to pay the agent for a replacement door. He and the lady move to the kitchen and are speaking in whispers. But even if they were right next to me, I wouldn't hear them. I can still only hear Rebecca's screams.

I hang my head and walk outside, through the broken-glass mess, hoping I'll get cut, too. My head is pounding. In the sunlight, black, yellow, and tan spots dance in front of my eyes. My shoes shuffle out to the edge of the pool, then

toward the shallow end and down the little steps. I sink in and taste chlorine. It's quiet and cold under the water.

Suddenly I'm coughing and choking as an arm yanks me out of the pool. Dad is pounding me on the back as I spit out the water I've swallowed.

"One of you is already in the hospital!" he hollers. "Take my jacket and put it around you, for God's sake."

"I killed her," I sob. "I wish I was never born."

"You didn't kill her," he cries, putting his arms around me. He hugs me tightly. "She'll be fine. It was an accident."

As we leave, the saleslady opens the front door for us. She has found her smile again and says, as if nothing's happened, "Please call with any questions." She hands Dad her card, clicks shut her handbag, locks the door behind us, and hustles away to her car.

Dad drives to the hospital. Mom is in the waiting room. "Rebecca has a broken nose but she is going to be fine. The emergency room doctors cleaned out her cuts and tomorrow a plastic surgeon is going to operate and she'll be getting a beautiful new nose."

"Can I see her?" I ask.

"No," says Mom sternly. "She's resting."

Does Mom think I'm going to play tag and chase Rebecca around the hospital?

"They gave her some sleeping medicine. I'll come back to the hospital later today," says Mom. "Let's go home now."

I slump in the backseat as we drive home. I didn't kill my sister and Mom says she's fine, but she's all alone and is going to be scared when she wakes up.

"Can I call Rebecca?" I ask in a small voice.

"She needs rest!" snaps Mom.

"We've never slept apart," I say.

"She'll do just fine without you, Rachel!" says Mom as we pull into the driveway.

That night as I go to sleep alone in our room for the first time, I stare at Rebecca's empty bed. In my dreams I imagine her leaving the hospital, covered in white bandages and wearing a white gown. She walks into our grocery store and grabs a shopping cart. There's a fruit section, a dairy section, and a nose section. Rebecca rolls her cart over to sample the noses. There are noses of famous people on display—Abraham Lincoln's nose, Napoleon's nose, and Marilyn Monroe's nose. Rebecca tries on many noses in front of a mirror. Some are big, some are tiny, and some even come with attached mustaches. Rebecca purchases Cleopatra's nose at the checkout counter. She removes the tag and wears her new nose out of the store.

Saturday I stay home with Blondie, who comes in just to look after me while Mom and Dad go to the hospital. Sunday we drop Mom at the hospital first thing and then come back later in the day to pick up her and Rebecca, who is ready to come home. No Hebrew school, no visits to grandparents today.

In my dream she looked much better. In real life she looks really gross. Between the many bandages, her face is swollen and puffy, especially around her eyes. She's wearing all new clothes and new shoes. Mom must have gone shopping for a new outfit.

Rebecca won't look at me. Mom and Dad walk on either side of her, holding her steady, as we make our way out of the smelly hospital to the car. I follow behind.

"I hate you," she whispers to me in the backseat once we are on the road. "How could you do this to me?"

She turns her head away, stares out the window, and sobs.

"Rachel, what did you do to Rebecca now?" cries Mom, whipping around from the front seat.

"Nothing," I answer, and stare at the back of my sister's wrapped head.

We don't speak until we go to our room.

"Stay away from me from now on, Rachel," she says.

"But it's not my fault," I protest. "You started the game."

"You didn't have to chase me through a glass door!" yells Rebecca. "You're the biggest idiot in the world and I'm not talking to you anymore!"

I am glad to go to school on Monday. My sister the mummy is home reading in bed.

In the morning, Mrs. Bunker is giving us a social studies lesson but I can't pay attention.

Instead, I watch Simone, the girl who is at the desk next to mine. Some of the kids call her "ghost girl," because her skin is as white as a sheet. Her eyes are icy blue and she has the lightest blond hair I've ever seen. She keeps a paste jar in her desk, and every day I watch her sneak it into her lap and take little bites from it. She's sick a lot and smells of pineapples, which makes me feel ill. Her hair is pulled tightly from her face in a ponytail.

My pencil moves across my notebook paper. A few minutes later I study my drawing and frown. Instead of a girl wearing a ponytail, Simone looks bald and about one hundred years old or maybe as old as Mrs. Bunker. I look back at Simone and see her face turning red. Has she seen my awful drawing? I crumple it up and slide it inside my desk. I glance back at Simone and see her face getting redder and redder.

"I'm sorry, Simone," I whisper. "Please forgive me."

She stares straight ahead and doesn't look at me. Her face is now as red as a ripe tomato.

Mrs. Bunker gazes in our direction and asks, "Simone, are you having a problem?"

Simone trembles and shakes her head. A tear rolls down her face. Mrs. Bunker marches over and says angrily, "Simone, you're going to have to leave the class."

I don't understand why Simone is in trouble and not me.

Mrs. Bunker hikes toward the door, tripping on her slip. The class laughs. Mrs. Bunker yanks her slip back up with both hands. "Come, Simone!" she commands. "I'm waiting."

Simone stands up. Her paste jar falls and splashes across the squares of mustard linoleum. The back of her dress is wet and wrinkly.

"Not a peep!" cries Mrs. Bunker. She pulls her handkerchief from her pocket and wipes her chin. Then she grabs Simone's hand and says, "We're going to the nurse's office, class. I'll be right back."

Strangely, the class stays silent while the teacher is gone. There's a pale yellow puddle on Simone's chair. The custodian arrives and washes up the mess. It all disappears and so does Simone, for the rest of the day.

Tuesday, Simone is back, but she isn't interested in talking to me or even looking in my direction. Big deal. I'm used to the silent treatment. But I'll never know if it was my drawing that caused her to lose control.

A week later, Rebecca's bandages are removed. Her black, blue, yellow, and purple face reminds me of kindergarten art projects.

During dinner, Mom announces, "The doctor says Rebecca's face is healing well," and smiles at her.

No one looks in my direction.

"Rebecca!" I cry that night. "Please speak to me."

She shakes her head and pretends to read *Stuart Little*.

Rebecca misses a week of school and no one cares because she's so smart. The second day after she returns, I hear Rebecca say to Georgie on the school bus, "I'm almost caught up."

Kids are staring at Rebecca on the bus. Most are quiet except Tony and Eddie. Tony hollers, "Rachel, why did you punch your sister? It can't be because she's ugly. Because you're just as ugly!" And he and Eddie snicker.

The jerks know it was an accident, because our teacher told them. I put my head in a book and ignore them.

On Sunday, Mom drives us to Hebrew school. "Rebecca," says Mom, "you're healing nicely, but I don't like the looks of that incision. The doctor says another operation will fix it."

Rebecca rubs her new nose. "Mom, it's almost invisible," says Rebecca, frowning.

"It is," I quickly agree.

Rebecca glares at me.

"We can wait and see," says Mom. "You can always have the operation later."

We wave goodbye, and walk separately into Mrs. Cohen's class.

"Today are chorus tryouts," Mrs. Cohen says. "Follow me to the music room."

A short, chubby man waves as we enter. He greets us and then tells us to form a line.

"My name is Mr. Otto. I want to hear each of you sing," he says, "one at a time."

He takes a seat at the piano, carefully tucks his stomach under the keys, and begins to play.

"Isn't Mr. Otto Dad's cousin?" I whisper to Rebecca.

She shakes her head, picks at her sweater, and moves a step away from me.

One by one our classmates sing.

I arrive at the front of the line. "Aren't you the Ringwood twins?" asks Mr. Otto, leaning over to see both of us.

We nod.

"You're so alike!" he observes. "You're like two cute little . . . cute little . . ."

Beavers, I think, giving him a toothy smile.

"Rabbits," he says. "No, I mean bunnies. Two cute little
bunny rabbits." He coughs. "Your father and I are third
cousins, you know. I bet you girls have beautiful voices like
mine," he says with a big smile. He plays a few notes.

"Do-re-mi-fa-so-la-ti-do," he sings. "Now, twins," he
exclaims, "repeat those notes one at a time." He points to
Rebecca and says, "You go first."

"Do-re-mi-fa-so-la-ti-do," she croaks.

"Stop!" he cries, looking like he's swallowed a palmetto
bug. "Now the other one," he says, pointing to me.

"Do-re-mi-fa-so-la-ti-do," I loudly croak.

"Well, that's enough! I'm not sure we share the same
gifts after all!" he broadcasts across the room. He massages
his throat with his fingers. "Please say hello to your dad.
Now, why don't you join your classmates in line?"

I'm smiling as Mr. Otto picks six other kids from class
for his chorus.

"Why are you so happy?" snaps Rebecca. "I wanted to
be picked for chorus."

"At least it's not my fault we croak like frogs!" I say.

12

Catwalk

Mom's on the warpath this morning. Dad's left on another trip. She's frowning and I'm at Custer's last stand.

I think Mom is mad because she and Dad decided not to
buy a new house. Maybe I ruined our chances. Maybe Dad's
afraid something even worse will happen if we look at any
more houses.

Mom's tired a lot lately. She spends hours in her room
with the curtains closed. When she comes out, she has dark
circles under her eyes and looks like she could use a rest all
over again. She goes crazy at the sight of muddy footprints

or uncombed hair. Rebecca and I carefully wipe our feet before we come inside and silently tiptoe about.

"This kitchen's dirty again!" Mom cries, wiping spilled milk from my breakfast bowl of cereal. Then she sprays down the whole counter and sponges it off. Ammonia fumes fill the air. "Blondie had this room spotless yesterday. It's time you girls made more of an effort around here. Especially since we aren't buying a new house. If you don't keep this place clean, it's going to crawl away. That's right—insects are going to carry it away! Do you girls hear me?"

I walk to the spotless refrigerator for a glass of orange juice.

"I just mopped the floor!" Mom yells. Her eyes shoot me dead.

I bet we have the cleanest house in Miami. Georgie's house is a comfy mess of cookie crumbs and cat hair. Our house is spotlessly clean. We could eat off our floors because Mom mops them every day.

"I want you twins to clean your closet after school," she says. "And, Rachel, you'll never attract a husband if you end up a hunchback. Stand up straight!"

In school today, Mrs. Bunker is talking about Lotta

Crabtree. She was a pretty little girl who sang and danced for the California gold miners. We read about the gold rush and then Mrs. Bunker asks us to write a paragraph on what we learned. I draw a picture of a dancing little girl. There are lumps of gold thrown at her feet and she's smiling. Mrs. Bunker walks around the room reading our paragraphs.

"Rachel," she says, wiping her chin with her handkerchief, "I wish you'd follow directions and *write* about the California gold rush. Now get started."

I watch her as she passes Simone's empty desk. Simone is out sick again.

The bus home from school is crowded. I see Rebecca sitting in the back with Georgie, but I would rather stand by myself if Rebecca isn't going to talk to me.

Tony, Eddie, and Crybaby Stevens get on and press toward me. I ignore them. I'm wondering what I would have done during the gold rush to entertain miners. I know I can't sing like Lotta Crabtree, because Mr. Otto didn't pick me for chorus. Mom and Dad are always criticizing how I look. I remember Mom's advice about standing up straight. I take a deep breath and roll back my shoulders. I move my elbows back and forth and step onto something lumpy. Crybaby Stevens whines and points to his toe. I look down, and next to his toe are two small mirrors rubberbanded to the tops of Tony Tombalo's penny loafers . . . and they're under my dress!

"You're trying to see my underwear!" I shout.

"We saw it!" says Eddie, giggling and snorting. "It's white!"

"You creep-heads!" I cry, lifting my Mary Janes and stomping the mirrors into tiny glass fragments.

I stare at the smashed mirrors and think about Rebecca covered with a million pieces of broken glass. I start to cry.

Eddie snickers as Tony jumps up and down on his smashed toes.

"You're both gross! I hate you!" I holler. I move away quickly to the front of the bus.

I wish I could disappear. I feel naked, but not the way the Tree Boys are naked. They're naked because everyone's naked in the jungle. No one's naked on this bus except me, and it's those boys' fault!

When the bus comes to our stop, I give Tony and Eddie dirty looks and run off. I walk in the opposite direction from our house.

"Where are you going?" growls Rebecca from behind me.

"The catwalk," I answer.

"Mom will go crazy if she finds out you went down there," she says.

"What do you care? I thought you weren't talking to me!" I yell, and walk three feet. I turn around hoping Rebecca is following, and she is.

"I can't let you go alone, Rachel," says Rebecca. "It's dangerous down there. But you're making me really mad."

"Like that's something new, Rebecca," I grumble.

We walk three blocks to the Garden of Eden Motel. Poor tourists who can't afford Miami Beach stay here. Pink paint is peeling from its walls and there's an empty swimming pool under repair in the back. GARDEN OF EDEN is written in green neon on the roof, but the letters GARDEN OF E are burned out. It blinks DEN MOTEL every night. I guess wild animals live inside.

The motel sits on a canal next to the highway. At the edge of the motel parking lot there are crumbling concrete stairs leading down to the catwalk. We found these stairs under some weeds a few years ago. The catwalk is a narrow concrete walkway sticking out from a rough rock wall. It runs alongside the canal for miles. We know this because we've tried to walk the length of it but have never been able to. Motorboats speed through the canal even though the signs say NO WAKE. The catwalk can be dangerous because waves from behind speeding boats can crash over it and knock you off balance and into the canal.

We climb down the stairs to the catwalk. Suddenly it's quiet and dark, while from above we hear rumbling sounds of traffic. The canal smells like used diapers. Garfish and barracuda are swimming in the fast current. Garfish look like small alligators that have become fish. Their needlelike teeth poke out of their mouths. Barracuda are a lot bigger and have many teeth, like fishy vampires. Some kids say they follow you for hours in the ocean like harmless dogs. But most kids in Miami brag about a cousin who's lost a finger or a toe to a barracuda. Rebecca and I have never met these fingerless cousins, but we won't swim anywhere near barracuda.

Farther down the catwalk we find two old black fishermen.

"Well, now, I think I am seeing double!" says the bigger one, who has a gold tooth and a broken straw hat.

The smaller one spits something brown into the canal and says, "They sure look alike."

"You girls twins?" asks the bigger one.

"Yes," we answer.

The men smile. I see that the smaller one is missing many teeth. I'm thinking I could loan him a few when Rebecca asks, "What are you fishing for?"

"Mullet," says the big one. "We use them for bait."

Small mullet are swimming in the canals, too. No one's afraid of mullet.

"You little girls better watch you're not eaten by a gator," says the bigger fisherman. "And that big barracuda down there by the rocks sure looks hungry."

It's a tough decision, being eaten by a barracuda or a mom. We decide to go home and wave goodbye to the fishermen. We're climbing up the stairs when Rebecca cries, "Look! There in the canal!"

A huge gray blob is rising out of the water. It dives down and its wide flat tail slaps the water.

"A manatee!" I exclaim.

"Do you think it's hungry?" asks Rebecca.

"At Oceanworld they threw lettuce to the manatees," I say. "They said they were also called sea cows because they graze on underwater pastures. Let's run home and get some greens."

"You're nuts!" cries Rebecca, chasing behind me back to the house. "You're going to get us in huge trouble. I'm not talking to you anyway."

Mom greets us at the door holding a big garbage bag. "It's about time you twins got home!" she exclaims huffily.

Rebecca gives me a slimy look.

We follow Mom to our closet. She points to stuff she

has decided is junk. "I'm getting rid of the wire hangers," she says. "Clothes look cheap and trashy on wire hangers."

Mom likes pretty fabric hangers. In minutes she has thrown away a torn pair of shoes, seven wire hangers, and a holey T-shirt. I see a furry tail sticking out of the garbage bag.

"Why is Lion-o in the trash?" I exclaim.

"It's time to throw the filthy thing out!" says Mom.

"There's nothing wrong with Lion-o," I say. "He needs a little surgery and rest."

"He stays in this bag," says Mom. "His stuffing is all over the floor."

She hands us sponges and ammonia. We wipe the tile floor of our closet clean.

"I'm going out," says Mom. "Blondie will be by shortly to babysit."

After Mom drives away, I race to the refrigerator and grab two heads of lettuce.

"Where do you think you're going?" asks Rebecca.

"You know," I remind her, and race out the front door.

"You make me so mad!" yells Rebecca, but she is running right behind me. We dash to the Garden of Eden and go down the stairs to the catwalk. We look up and down the canal and easily spot the manatee partly submerged on

the far side. We tear the lettuce into small pieces and throw it in the water. The manatee is growing bigger and bigger as it swims toward us. It must be ten feet long! Its body is shaped like a giant walrus. It has two paddle-shaped front flippers but no legs. Its face is wrinkled and covered with stiff whiskers. Before eating, the manatee lifts its head above the water and watches us.

"Hello, Mr. Manatee," I say. It dips toward the lettuce and takes a bite. Suddenly, we hear the roar of a motor-boat. We see one coming up the canal, from where we'd seen the fishermen.

"It's coming this way!" I scream. "And it might run over the manatee!"

"Slow down! Slow down!" we yell at the small craft, waving our hands in the air and pointing toward the water. "Don't hurt it!"

The man at the controls sees us just in time and cuts his engine. The boat's wake rushes over the catwalk. We hold tightly to the rough rock walls and get soaked. I spit out canal water and shake my hair. Rebecca rubs water out of her eyes.

"What's wrong?" the man calls.

We point and cry, "Manatee!"

He finally sees the creature, smiles, and shouts his

thanks. The three of us watch as the manatee slowly swims in the direction the boat was coming from. When the boat starts up and leaves, we see the black fishermen walking toward us and pointing in the departed manatee's direction.

"Haven't seen hide nor hair of one of them in a long while," says the man with missing teeth.

"They bring good luck," says the other man, looking over our dripping-wet clothes. "And it looks like you girls could use some."

"We saved a manatee!" I sing as we walk home. "Maybe we can come down to feed it every day and make it our pet."

"Mom doesn't allow pets," says Rebecca. Then she stops. "Oh, no. How will we explain two missing heads of lettuce?"

"Maybe Blondie will think of something to tell Mom," I say hopefully.

We walk up the steps and into the house. Blondie is in the kitchen cooking dinner.

"Where have you been?" she asks, crossing her arms over her enormous chest. "And why are your clothes and shoes so muddy?"

"Ask the troublemaker," says Rebecca, pointing at me.

I tell Blondie the whole story.

"Well, I guess it was a good thing you were there to save that poor manatee. But I don't think your parents would be happy to hear you were on that catwalk. Let's make a deal. If you promise not to go back there, I'll brag to your parents about the powerful hunger for salad you had tonight."

We both give her a hug and run to get ourselves cleaned up.

We return wearing pajamas and eat dinner.

"Why is the stereo on in the living room?" asks Rebecca as we do the dishes under Blondie's supervision.

"After we finish in here, I'm teaching you girls the twist!" explains Blondie. "I brought some records tonight."

"I already know how to twist," I say as I rinse a plate.

"Bigmouth knows how to do everything," says Rebecca, taking it from me and getting busy with a towel.

"That's no way to speak to your sister," scolds Blondie. "Now, Rachel, you think you know how to dance? You can show me what you know in a few minutes."

Finally the dishes are done, the table is wiped off, and the floor is mopped clean. In the living room Blondie puts on a new record and I show her my moves. At first Rebecca just watches while sitting next to Blondie, but soon she

jumps off the couch and joins me. I can tell by Blondie's face we're not twisters.

"You white girls ain't got no soul!" says Blondie. "Get loose as a goose."

Blondie stands up. "Here, girls, watch me twist to Chubby Checker!"

Blondie's moves are smooth, though she's as big as a tow truck. As the record repeats, she works with us and we get pretty good, too. It's the most fun I've had with my sister for a long time.

"I'm as hot as a sweet potato fresh out of the oven!" cries Blondie as the song is about to start again.

"Put something else on," I say. "I have soul!"

Blondie puts on James Brown and I twist to the floor. I lie down on the cold tiles. I move my arms and legs in the air. I jump up and wiggle and waggle. I shimmy. I shake. I twist hard and slam into dancing Rebecca, who knocks Mom's Italian glass vase to the floor. What is it with me and breaking glass?

The fun is over and it's my fault again. I know that Rebecca thinks I'm an idiot and I'm about to cry. Now would be a good time for me to vanish. I bet Mom will wish I could disappear.

"Nobody move," calls Blondie, who runs and gets a

broom. Quickly she sweeps the broken glass pieces from around our feet. "Now you girls go to bed. I shouldn't have let you get so carried away. And don't worry, I'll take care of things with your mom."

I look gratefully at Blondie. She nods and says, "Now go!"

My punishment for breaking the vase isn't bad, it turns out. I have garbage duty for one month. The first thing I do is find Lion-o in Mom's bag of giveaways and return him to my bed. I hide him under my pillow.

13
Alligators

In school, Mrs. Bunker announces, "It's late fall and I feel a crispness in the air!"

We stare at her because it's early morning and already hot.

"I know it's a little warm today, but the weather's getting cooler and there are fewer mosquitoes. Many of you will be visiting the Everglades this winter," she says. "Have any of you seen an alligator?"

Everybody raises a hand.

"What happens if an alligator loses a tooth?" she asks.

Pinky Greene's hand shoots up.

Pinky and I are slowly becoming friends. She sits behind me but we never really talked until yesterday, when I knocked into her by accident at the pencil sharpener. Before I could apologize, she pushed me back. I shoved her. She punched me. I punched her back. She pinched my arm. I pinched her hand. We stared at each other and started laughing.

"Yes, young lady?" asks Mrs. Bunker.

"It grows another," says Pinky.

Mrs. Bunker nods and continues. "Should we be afraid of alligators?"

Everyone is afraid of alligators in *The Tree Boys* except Big Hippo. Alligators can't bite through Big Hippo's thick skin. Dad says alligators eat children and pets and lurk in the canals that run behind our houses. Sometimes after rainstorms, alligators are found in swimming pools. Kids say gators run across the golf courses at night.

"I'm afraid of alligators," I say out loud.

"You don't have to be afraid," whispers Pinky. "All you have to do is cover its eyes and get it on its back."

"How do you do that?" I ask in a low voice.

Mrs. Bunker waves her handkerchief at me and says, "Rachel, perhaps you'd like to teach class today."

"No, thank you, Mrs. Bunker," I reply.

At lunch Pinky drops her tray next to mine and says, "I bet you've never eaten gator, have you?"

I scrunch my nose and answer, "No! Have you?"

"Yeah, lots of times," she replies.

"Does it taste fishy?" I ask. I think about the red snapper Mom bakes when Granny Fanny's neighbors bring home a catch to share. Everyone's happy to eat it but me.

"It tastes like fried chicken," says Pinky. "I know a lot about alligators from my grandfather. He's a Miccosukee Indian chief and lives in the Everglades."

"My grandpa lives on Miami Beach," I say. I wish he were an Indian chief. I imagine Pinky and her grandfather paddling a canoe while tribesmen onshore bow and throw orchids.

The next day, Pinky asks me if I want to meet her grandfather. I nod and smile like an eager beaver. That night at dinner I ask my parents, who say it's okay to arrange a date for Saturday. Rebecca gives me a strange look from her side of the table.

I call Pinky that night and our mothers talk. Her mom is going to come get me at my house Saturday afternoon.

But things work out a little differently. On Saturday morning Mom takes us shopping, and we get home just in time to meet Pinky's mom.

"I have a headache," Mom says while waving at the car parked in our driveway. "Rebecca, you go spend the day with Rachel and her little friend."

"I don't want to," whines Rebecca.

"Go!" she says, and marches into the house.

"Hello, I'm Mrs. Greene," says Pinky's mom, sticking her head out the car window.

I explain that my sister's coming, too.

"That's just fine," says Mrs. Greene.

Pinky says hello to both of us as we crawl into the backseat. I guess she and Rebecca know each other from school, too.

"You two sure look alike!" Pinky exclaims as she leans over from the front seat. "It must be the best thing in the world to have a twin sister. Who's older?" she asks.

"Rebecca's older by two minutes," I explain.

Rebecca glares out her window and says, "I'll trade places with you anytime, Pinky."

No one says anything for a while, and then I ask, "Pinky, how come you live in Miami and not in the Everglades with your grandfather?"

"Pinky's only part Miccosukee," says her mom, chuckling. "We prefer to live in Miami. Pinky's grandfather, Mr. Tiger, married my mother many, many years ago. Pinky

never met her grandmother. She died before Pinky was born."

After a long drive down the Tamiami Trail into the Everglades, we park behind a wooden fence. "Come this way," says Mrs. Greene as she opens a gate. We walk on a path to a footbridge across a canal. On the other side sit a cluster of chikee huts and some banana trees on an island surrounded by an endless sea of water and green grass.

We studied chikee huts in school. The Miccosukee Indians live in chikee huts because of the hot and humid south Florida weather. The huts have no electricity or running water. They are built on cypress log frames and their roofs are woven palm fronds. A little girl wearing beads around her neck runs past a small palm tree and disappears inside a chikee.

"How does anyone get around in the Everglades?" I ask.

"Airboat," says Pinky. "And some people use cypress canoes."

A large dark bird flaps over our heads.

"That's an anhinga," says Mrs. Greene.

"What kind of swamp critters live out there?" asks Rebecca, pointing beyond the huts where the green stretches forever toward the blue sky.

"There are many turtles, snakes, raccoon, deer, and alligators," says Pinky.

A large, tan-colored old man with white hair walks out of a chikee hut and waves.

"Here's Grandfather!" exclaims Pinky. He's wearing a jacket made from a million bright stripes.

"Come on up," he says. We climb the wooden steps to his hut and he shakes our hands.

"I like your colorful jacket," I say.

"We call it patchwork," says Mr. Tiger, leading us inside.

It's dark and cool in the hut. "Your grandfather has natural air-conditioning," I say.

Three women with black hair are wearing capelike blouses and wide floor-length skirts like Mr. Tiger's jacket. Around their necks are colorful beaded necklaces. They're sitting at pedal-powered sewing machines, picking up bright little squares of fabric from large grass baskets and sewing them together. One woman with shiny black eyes smiles as I watch her work on a sleeve for a jacket like Mr. Tiger's. I'm thinking chikee huts are nice, until I see a giant palmetto bug crawling on the floor. Rebecca slaps her forehead as mosquitoes buzz her face. "Mom would have a conniption living in a chikee hut," I whisper to Rebecca.

"To the wrestling pit," says Pinky's grandfather. He leads us into the hot sunshine and behind the chikees. A black butterfly with pale yellow stripes flutters by.

"Please stand behind this wooden fence," Mr. Tiger says.

Pinky's mom points and says, "My dad has a surprise. Your friends are going to see Billie wrestle an alligator."

On the other side of the fence is a circle of dirt. Billie is dark-skinned and has short, straight black hair. He wears black pants and a jacket just like Mr. Tiger's.

"Go ahead, Billie," calls Mr. Tiger.

Billie lifts a latch on a door, and a gator as fast as lightning kicks through the dirt and tries to take a mouthful of his feet.

Rebecca and I gasp. I bet that thing's six feet long.

Billie steps back and it thrashes its greenish-gray tail back and forth at his legs. I think the gator's trying to trip Billie so it can bite his head off. Billie grabs its snapping jaws and forces them shut between his big hands. He turns the gator over on its back and pets it on the belly. The ferocious animal stops moving. Has it fallen asleep? Billie flips the gator over. It springs to life and tries to sink its teeth into Billie as he jumps out of the pen.

I'm leaning and resting my arm on top of the wooden fence. "That was really scary," I say to Pinky.

Her grandfather grabs me and swings me in the air.

I yelp.

"Watch where you put your hands and arms, little miss!" he says sternly.

Hissss!

I turn and see the gator snapping its teeth right where my hand was dangling seconds before.

"Has the sun French-fried your brain?" Rebecca cries.

"Everything's all right!" says Mrs. Greene, patting my arm. "Let's get out of the sun and stop for a cold drink and snack."

Mr. Tiger says, "I'll meet you in a minute to say good-bye."

We walk back over the bridge. Mrs. Greene and Pinky stand in front of the car talking. Rebecca and I climb to safety in the backseat. Mr. Tiger walks swiftly toward us. He's carrying something in bright vivid colors. He hugs Mrs. Greene and Pinky goodbye. He sticks his head in the back window and says, "I would like you to have this because you were almost nipped and now join a long line of Micco-sukees who have tangled with gators."

He hands me a jacket just like his but in a small size.

"Thank you," I say, relieved that he's smiling and not angry.

That night, I wear my new colorful jacket to dinner.

"Where did you get that?" asks Dad. "Isn't it Seminole Indian?"

"It's Miccosukee. My girlfriend's grandfather gave it to me," I say, watching Rebecca, who's frowning.

"The girls spent the day with a friend in the Everglades," says Mom.

"I would love to sell those jackets to my customers," says Dad.

Rebecca looks really upset.

"That might also help out the tribe," says Mom.

I smile and get up from the table.

Rebecca says, "You'd look really dumb with one arm!" and follows me out of the kitchen.

"One arm?" asks Dad.

"Nothing!" I grumble as we walk to our room.

"At least no one would confuse me with you anymore," I want to say to her. But I don't.

14

Manners

"Thanksgiving's almost here," says Mom, "and this year I want you twins to have better table manners. You will be taking lessons at a charm school that's opening tonight in downtown Miami."

Across the living room Blondie chuckles as she sprays the coffee table with lemon-scented polish.

"Why do we need better manners?" I ask. "We don't have Thanksgiving like other families. They have it at home with lots of happy relatives. They eat turkey, pass cranberry sauce, and compliment the cook for all the good food. We go to a restaurant. Aunt Florence complains about the waiters. Granny Fanny tells her to have good thoughts. And Dad yells at everyone to calm down."

"Thank you, Rachel, for your stunning character assassination of my family," snarls Mom, walking to her bedroom and slamming the door.

"Character assassination?" I ask. Rebecca ignores me.

Dad's out of town again and Mom seems especially unhappy this time. He gave her a worried look before he left. She's sleeping till noon and complains that she's tired when she wakes.

"You girls aren't the only ones who could use some charm school," says Blondie. We laugh nervously.

Rebecca looks around in case Mom's spying on us. "I bet we have to go because Rachel parks her elbows on the table," she snaps.

"No, I don't!" I say.

Why is Rebecca so mean? Is she going to be mad at me forever?

After dinner, Mom supervises as we put on nice outfits. Before long she's driving us downtown at top speed and is suddenly pulling up in front of a tall office building.

"Charm school's upstairs," says Mom. "I'll pick you up in an hour."

I want to ask her if she knows for sure that she has

the pickup time right, but I keep my mouth shut for once.

"See you later," Mom yells, and floors the gas as if she's on the run from the charm police.

A man in the lobby tells us to take an elevator to the top floor. Even before the doors open, we hear fancy music. We walk into a brightly lit room full of dancing children. They look like princes and princesses waltzing in a fairy tale.

"Come in," says a frowning woman who looks more like a witch than Rebecca did in her Halloween costume. "We're about to finish our last dance," she scowls. "You're late!"

She takes our names and checks them off a list. Her dress has a big bow on it. She reminds me of a badly wrapped present.

"We're sorry," says Rebecca in her most polite voice. "Our mom just dropped us off."

"You'll have to catch up next week. We conclude our evenings by eating punch and cookies with savoir faire," says the witch.

"Save-the-fair?" I ask.

The witch starts to say something, then stops, shakes her head, and walks away.

"Look over there!" I whisper. I can't believe my eyes. On

a side table sit millions of cookies on giant pink serving plates! Cookies of all kinds!

"Hold it, Rachel," Rebecca says, grabbing my arm. "Are you trying to get us into trouble?"

She's right. I restrain myself. We stand against the wall watching the dancers and feeling foolish. But the more I look, the more I can see that few of the dancers really know what they are doing. They trip, step on each other's toes, bump into other couples, and move stiffly. Maybe they feel foolish, too.

Then the music and dancing stop and the princes and princesses turn into ordinary kids, greedy for save-the-fair. Suddenly kids are racing by us in a mad rush to the cookie table. I'm running, too, right behind them.

"No running!" yells the witch. "Walk like ladies and gen-tlemen."

No one listens as we shove our way to the table. I grab a napkin and place one cookie on top of another, building a sugar mountain. When I have as many as I can balance, I slowly make my way to a chair. I grab a chocolate chip cookie and shove it in my mouth, then realize I forgot punch.

"Watch my cookies!" I say to my sister as I hand her my pile.

"Hurry up," says Rebecca, standing by my chair, holding my cookies, as well as a napkin with four small cookies of her own.

I return with my punch, and the witch is saying to Rebecca, "You're a piggy little girl hogging all these cookies."

"But—" cries Rebecca.

The woman shouts, "Silence, please. Now, where's the newspaperman!"

A man with a camera runs over.

"Take a photo of this greedy girl next to her well-mannered sister," she says, pointing at us.

Instantly, we're blinded by a bright light as the camera flashes.

Rebecca screams, "That's not fair!" The cookies all fall to the floor.

"Don't talk back to me!" says the witch. "In fact, I would like your nice sister to escort you out of here. You two can wait outside for your mother."

The other kids are eating their cookies and watching the commotion. I grab Rebecca's arm and pull her out the door. The silent treatment is already under way as we wait for the elevator.

Downstairs, we walk to the sidewalk and sit on a bus bench.

"It's my fault I got you into another mess," I say. "And I'm going to get you out of it."

I will, too. Rebecca gives me a doubtful look, but I already know what I can do.

Soon Mom's car roars to a stop and we climb in.

"How was it?" she asks.

The backseat of the car is silent.

"Learning proper manners must be tiring for girls who need to be taught so much," says Mom.

In the morning, Rebecca is still giving me the silent treatment.

As we fix our breakfast at the counter Mom hollers from the breakfast table, "Look here in *The Miami Herald*. There's a photo of you two at charm school last night!"

We run and look at our picture in the paper. The caption reads, "Identical in everything but manners," and then goes on to talk about the opening of the charm school. The girl in the photo holding the cookie skyscraper is correctly identified as Rebecca, while I'm the polite princess holding just a cup of punch.

"Rebecca," asks Mom, "what on earth were you thinking?"

My sister flashes me an angry look, but I'm ready to put my plan into action.

"No!" I say. "They made a mistake. You know . . . because we're twins. That's me with the cookies. Rebecca's the one with the punch."

Luckily the photo's a little blurry and hard to see. Rebecca's eyes are as big as the grapefruit she's about to eat.

"Well, that figures." Mom chuckles. "Did you girls enjoy last night?"

This time it's Rebecca who comes to the rescue. "No!" she says, and explains how mean the lady was.

"Well," says Mom, "for that kind of money, I'm not making you go unless you want to. And since the paper mentions that one of my daughters has good manners, I guess she can help out my other daughter. Right?"

We both nod and smile politely.

We keep our elbows off the table on Thanksgiving a couple of weeks later. Aunt Florence doesn't eat turkey. She has to be original and order a T-bone, well done. Then she yells at the red-faced waiter to "take a hike" when he brings her an overcooked steak. Granny Fanny is angry because they serve really good baked apples. Dad assures her a million times that her apples are better. Mom stands up with a throbbing headache and knocks over a waiter's tray as he is serving pumpkin pie to another table. There is plenty of bad behavior, but not from us twins.

15
Christmas

It's almost Christmas, and before lunch one day Mrs. Bunker asks for a volunteer to sing "Silent Night" so the class can hear the words.

My arm takes charge and shoots into the air. Mrs. Bunker gives me a nod.

I slowly stand up and begin to sing happily in my croaking voice, "Silent night, holy night . . ."

I know all the verses, but Mrs. Bunker stops me after the first. Now the whole class stands up and sings along with me from the top.

Tonight is actually the first night of Chanukah. There

are two Jewish kids in our class. I'm one and Sara Fine is the other. I don't know her too well. For one thing, she goes to the other temple in our neighborhood.

After the Christmas carol, we take our seats and Mrs. Bunker says, "Jewish people are celebrating Chanukah this week. Rachel and Sara, would either of you like to tell us about your holiday?"

We shake our heads and sit lower in our seats.

She explains that Chanukah is the celebration of the victory of Judas Maccabaeus over the mean Antiochus, who put idols in the Temple and ordered the Jews not to worship their God. After the Temple was cleaned of idols, there was only a one-day supply of oil, but the Temple lamp burned for eight days and nights, until new jars of clean oil were found. Jews light a menorah for eight nights to honor this miracle.

Carlos Hernandez raises his hand and says, "Jews are lucky. I heard they get presents every night of Chanukah. That means eight nights of presents instead of one like the rest of us!"

Not at my house. Rebecca and I light the Chanukah candles and say the prayer for eight nights, but we don't get presents. We usually get something only the first night from Mom and Dad. They just hover around the other

nights while Rebecca and I take turns lighting the menorah and saying the prayer. When it's my turn to do the prayer I slowly say, *"Baruch ata, Adonai, Eloheinu melech haolam,"* and then the rest really fast so no one knows I can't remember half of it. Rebecca usually butts in and finishes the prayer for me.

Granny Fanny doesn't celebrate Chanukah, but she likes to drop by with Aunt Florence each year for one of the nights.

By the third night Rebecca and I are exchanging Life Savers and sticks of gum and singing our favorite holiday song, "I Have a Little Dreidel":

I have a little dreidel
I made it out of clay
And when it's dry and ready
Then dreidel I shall play.

Oh, dreidel, dreidel, dreidel
I made it out of clay
Oh, driedel, dreidel, dreidel
Now dreidel we shall play.

There's more to this song, but we stop here every time and crack up into a laughing fit. A dreidel is a four-sided spinning top for children to play with during the holiday. Sometimes we are given chocolate ones at Hebrew school.

My favorite Chanukah tradition is Blondie's sizzling potato pancakes called latkes, which are fried in oil because that celebrates the miracle oil that burned for eight days. Blondie serves them with Granny Fanny's homemade applesauce. I like this tradition because we're not usually allowed to eat fried food and latkes taste great.

I'll still trade Carlos Chanukah for Christmas, though. I love Christmas. I love the colored lights wrapped around palm trees. I love the smell of real Christmas trees for sale on the empty lot near our house. I love eggnog even if Mom says it's fattening. I love tinsel even if it doesn't look like icicles. I love the fancy wrapped packages heaped under Christmas trees. I love how everyone's happy, especially families.

During lunch, Georgie tells our table that a kid told her the whole school's getting a Christmas present. "It's going to snow today after school," she says.

"Whoever said that is an idiot!" says Pinky. "It's warm and sunny outside."

"And the sky is bright blue," I say, pointing to the window.

Tony runs over and shouts, "Snow, snow! Snow is coming."

I know he's a jerk but I wonder what everyone is talking about.

The word *snow* is repeated over and over in the cafeteria. By the time we walk back to class it's flying through the hallways like a blizzard.

Everyone's whispering and no one is listening to Mrs. Bunker.

"Class, please quiet down," says Mrs. Bunker. "We have an icy surprise for you today!" She giggles and pats her chin with her handkerchief.

We stop talking and pay attention.

"We aren't having a snowstorm this afternoon, but snow made and donated by a local ice company is being piled in the driveway as I speak. We're letting everyone out a little early to play in it before the buses and your parents arrive."

Everyone starts screaming. Tony rips up a piece of notebook paper into tiny bits and throws it over his head.

"If you want to see snow, you do need to be quiet until the bell rings," says Mrs. Bunker.

There's so much squealing, rumbling, and stamping of feet you'd think the dump trucks were coming through our classroom. Mrs. Bunker keeps the racket to a quiet roar until the bell rings and we escape through the door and tear down the hallways.

There's a huge pile of icy white stuff in front of the school. The sun is shining and cool light-blue water is melting off its edges. Lots of kids are running through it, throwing and kicking it into the air. Crybaby Stevens is making a tiny snowman. Rebecca and Georgie race by and jump in.

"Snow!" I cry, and kick it. It's hard and icy. I thought snow was soft and fluffy.

Eddie and Tony toss a lump at me and laugh. I walk to the other side of the pile and pick up a chunk of snow. I throw it into the air straight above my head. It comes down and flattens Crybaby Stevens's snowman. He starts to cry.

"Apologize, Rachel," my sister says.

"I'm sorry," I say.

"You should win the biggest-troublemaker-in-the-world award," says Rebecca. "Come on, Georgie's mom is driving us home."

I'm glad. I'm already fed up with snow. The real stuff. But not the fake stuff.

There's a ton of fake snow sprayed, sprinkled, and scattered all over the mall as our family goes shopping a few

days later. Christmas is next week and every store window is speckled with the white stuff. We pass a giant Christmas tree covered with white snow globs. It's decorated with tiny blinking lights and colorful Christmas ornaments. It's so beautiful! I wish we could take it home and put it in our house. "No Christmas trees," grumbles Dad whenever I ask. "We're Jews, we're not like other people," he says.

He's right. We're nothing like the happy families racing by carrying bags and bags of brightly wrapped presents. They're planning the biggest and best party of the year and we're not invited. Christmas music blares from every open doorway as we walk through the mall.

For my family, shopping means we wander for hours while Mom tries on clothes. Now we're heading to the big department store. A man on the left side of the entrance is ringing a bell and collecting donations for charity in a big black pot. On the right, a choral group in red and green sweaters sings "Joy to the World." We walk between them and go into the store.

I poke Rebecca in the side and say, "I bet those singers are sweating in those outfits."

She ignores me and shakes her head at the grinning lady trying to spray her with perfume. Mom stops in front of the aisle marked BETTER SPORTSWEAR. I hold my breath hoping we don't enter, but we do. She walks forward and grabs three mostly black short-sleeved cotton dresses from a rack. She holds them to her chest in front of a nearby mirror and looks miserable.

"What's wrong?" asks my father.

"I'm too fat to wear these dresses," she snaps.

"Didn't you say black makes a woman look thin?" he asks with a big sheepish grin.

She shakes her head and goes into a dressing room to try them on. Dad sits nearby on a chair and reads a newspaper.

Groups of kids are running toward a sign that reads THE NORTH POLE. It's not fair. I've never sat on Santa's lap. And now I'm probably too old.

"Dad," I ask, "can I sit on Santa's lap?"

"*No!* And that spells N-O!" he grumbles.

I follow two boys past the jewelry-and-watch counter and arrive at Santa's house. A long line of children waits by a red velvet rope. The rope is attached to two red-and-white-striped poles. An elf lifts the rope for each child to visit Santa. Santa is sitting on a white chair in front of a house. I sneak closer and see that Santa looks like a chubby woman with a beard. I wonder what the real Santa would say about this impostor.

A sled and mechanical reindeer are parked nearby. The reindeer lift their heads up and down. Rudolph is first with his red blinking nose.

*Ho-ho-ho*s fill the air and then the click of a camera as an elf takes a photo of every child who sits on Santa's lap.

I race back and find Rebecca spinning a rack of ladies' flower-print pants.

"I know where you've been," she says.

I feel my face turning as red as Rudolph's nose. I creep to Dad's chair and sit next to him on the carpet. I wonder if the Tree Boys hung up little red and green stockings in their tree house. Maybe they never heard of Santa. Impossible, I think, everyone's heard of Santa!

The dressing room curtain rips open and Mom twirls in a black-and-lime-striped dress.

"You look beautiful, Eve," says Dad. "Girls, tell your mother she looks beautiful."

"You look beautiful, Mom," we repeat as she examines herself in the mirror. She decides she will take the dress and returns to the dressing room to change.

Dad pays for the dress and the clerk asks, "Would you like this gift-wrapped?"

Dad shakes his head.

"Merry Christmas!" cries the clerk after ringing up the sale. She hands Rebecca and me each a candy cane.

We walk behind Mom and Dad past the jingling, jangling, and *ho-ho-ho!* sounds of Christmas, licking our candy treats.

It turns out that I'm not the only one who's curious about Santa. On Christmas Eve, I wake up in the middle of the night. I hear a rustle from Rebecca's bed. In the moonlight, I watch her dig out from under her animal army. She tiptoes to the sock drawer and pulls out a napkin covering something. Carefully she sneaks out. I count to five and follow her. A light goes on in the kitchen as she opens the refrigerator door. I hover against the edge of the doorframe watching her pour a glass of milk. She softly shuts the refrigerator door. I quickly step away into darkness. She's walking through the living room toward the fireplace. Rebecca sets the glass of milk on the bricks in front of our fireplace and opens the napkin. She carefully removes something and places it by the milk.

"What are you doing?" I whisper.

Rebecca opens her mouth wide. She's going to scream.

"Shhhh! It's me, Rachel."

"What are *you* doing here?" she asks.

"What do you mean, what am I doing here?" I exclaim. "What are you doing here?"

"Rachel, please don't tell on me," cries Rebecca. "Dad will never forgive me if he finds out."

"Finds out what?" I ask.

She faintly mumbles, "I'm waiting for Santa."

"Santa!" I cry.

"Shut up!" she whispers, and covers my mouth with her hand. She takes a deep breath and heaves a sigh. "Santa might visit if you put out milk and cookies. He's thirsty and hungry from his long journey."

"He is?" I speak softly. "How do you know?"

"Everyone says so," answers Rebecca.

"Rebecca, have you waited for Santa before?" I ask.

"I try every year," she utters. "I wake up early Christmas morning and remove the untouched milk and cookies before anyone sees them."

"You do?" I ask. "But you never told me."

"I was afraid to tell you. You might have told Dad," says Rebecca. "He'd be furious. You know how he is about this stuff."

"Don't worry," I say, frowning at her remark. "I won't tell, but why are apricot rugalach on that napkin? Wouldn't Santa prefer chocolate chip cookies or Oreos?"

"He might like to try something Jewish," says Rebecca. "They're cookies, too!"

"Where did you get the rugalach?" I ask.

"Granny Fanny's," says Rebecca.

I run and get my blanket and Lion-o. I wrap the blanket around us and place Lion-o nearby to stand guard. Rebecca snivels and says, "Thank you for not saying I'm too old to believe in Santa."

She yawns and falls asleep. My rear end is sore from sitting on the tile floor. "It's really late," I say, and softly shake her. She stands up and I lead her to bed.

In the morning, I run to the fireplace. There are no signs of Santa or of the milk and rugalach.

Rebecca's alone in the kitchen, drinking orange juice and looking at the newspaper's funny pages.

"You know who . . . didn't come last night," she says, and winks. "Here, have this." She hands me a rugalach.

"Merry Christmas, Rebecca," I say.

"Merry Christmas, Rachel," she says.

We're eating when Dad walks in. He pours a large glass of milk and says, "Mom isn't feeling well. Come into our bedroom and kiss her good morning."

We follow Dad to their bedroom. Dad hands her the

glass of milk and she takes a sip. Mom's hair is a mess. Her white lace nightgown is all wrinkly.

"I don't want to live," says Mom. "I want to die."

I freeze as Mom stares past me with icy-blue eyes.

"What's wrong, Mom?" asks Rebecca.

"Go away, children," says Mom. "I wish you—"

"That's enough, Eve!" says Dad. "Go finish your breakfast, girls." He pushes us out of their bedroom.

"Mom hates us," I say.

"No, she doesn't," says Rebecca. "She's just depressed."

"Maybe she's sad because everyone in the world is happy on Christmas," I reply.

We look miserably at each other.

Dad walks into the kitchen, claps his hands like his father, and says, "Let's go to a movie!"

Soon we're back at the mall, at a James Bond movie. But it's hard to enjoy the movie knowing Mom's lying in bed. Afterward, Dad walks ahead while Rebecca and I stay close behind. We drive home in silence, and a fully dressed Mom opens the door. Her cherry-red lipstick is smiling bright. She's fine now.

16
Temple

Dad's suitcases are by the front door again and he's ready to take his first sales trip of the new year. Mom fake-smiles as we hug him goodbye.

"Study hard while I'm away," he says, carrying his suitcases to his car. "That means you, Rachel. And have a nice time at temple today."

"I'll get dressed and be right out, girls," says Mom after he leaves. She straightens her robe.

Rebecca and I climb into the hot car. We wait forever. We each clutch a fuzzy sweater from Granny Fanny. I'm carrying my new wicker monkey bag. On the last night of Chanukah, Dad gave us the choice of either the monkey bag or a beach hat with built-in plastic sunglasses. Luckily Rebecca chose the hat. I loved the monkey bag the first moment I saw it.

Mom finally slides into the front seat and her car shoots down the street like a speeding bullet. It rained hard last night and we crash through shallow rivers of black water. She drops us at the curb in front of the temple and zooms away at a million miles an hour.

We jump across a big puddle and land on the walkway in front of the door. The Arctic tundra lies ahead so I put on my pink sweater. It scratches my neck, and its shiny lining feels like plastic wrap as it slides up and down my clammy back. Rebecca shoves herself into her blue sweater and frowns. Her face is red and sweaty from the jungle heat.

My monkey purse rocks back and forth as we work open the heavy front door. It's like pulling a giant rock away from the entrance to a cave. It slowly gives as we pull it open with all our strength. Freezing air rushes out. I stop and button my sweater to the top. Rebecca lets go of the door and it slams shut on monkey's head!

"His head is crushed!" I cry, prying him out.

"We're late!" she complains. "Haven't you noticed there's no one around?"

Monkey's head is smashed and one of his black plastic eyes has fallen out. I want to drop to the floor to look for it but Rebecca grabs me.

"Come on!" she says. And we run down the checkered hallway to class.

"Tardy again, girls?" notes Mrs. Cohen with a frown.

Rebecca glares at me like it's my fault. We quickly take seats. Rhonda Wolf and Susie Rabinowitz are laughing and pointing at my poor purse. They think it belongs in the garbage can.

Mrs. Cohen is talking about prophets. One lives in a cave in a hot, dry desert. I would like to go there right now. To hide and to get warm. I'm shivering. Rebecca's shivering, too. She's holding the top of her sweater tightly around her throat. The air-conditioning is blasting through white vents directly above our heads. I look around the room. Everyone looks comfortable but us.

A teacher named Miss Wilde walks in. She's wearing a rainbow-striped sweater.

Someone else is freezing around here.

She whispers something into Mrs. Cohen's ear.

"Go ahead and ask the class," says Mrs. Cohen.

"I need someone to help with the bulletin board out-side the younger kids' classroom," she says. "Our theme is Noah's ark."

My arm takes control and shoots into the air. The lining inside my sleeve slides down and bunches up. I've got to get out of here, and so I wave my arm wildly.

Miss Wilde picks me! It's a MIRACLE! I pull down my sweater sleeve, grab my broken purse, and follow her out the door. She puts her hand on my shoulder and we walk the black-and-white-checkered hallway to heaven.

We stop at a table of art supplies in front of the hall-way bulletin board. In her classroom I hear her kids busy with the music teacher. Miss Wilde hands me a pile of con-struction paper, Magic Markers, and a pair of scissors, and we get busy. She cuts Noah's ark out of brown paper while I cut out waves of water from light blue and dark blue paper.

"Rachel, why don't you draw some pairs of animals for the ark?" she suggests. "Here are photos of various animals. Use them for reference."

"What's this?" I ask, pointing to a big furry red monkey.

"That's an orangutan," she says.

I draw two frogs, two zebras, and two orangutans.

"You're doing a great job," she says, magically creating two ostriches from black and white paper.

"But my animals aren't good enough to go on the ark," I reply.

"Why not?" she exclaims. "It's not a private club. It's Noah's ark. Anyway, your animals are charming! I love the naïve quality of young artists."

"The what?" I ask.

"Watch me draw, Rachel," says Miss Wilde, picking up a black marker.

I watch as she draws a perfect Noah.

"How do you draw like that?" I ask.

"Practice, Rachel," she explains. "Practice every day and I know you'll be a good artist someday."

We work happily together for a while, then it's time for both of us to get back to our classrooms.

"I hope you won't mind coming and helping me again," says Miss Wilde.

I love temple! I smile and skip to class for the last hour of Hebrew school.

"Sit down, Rachel," Mrs. Cohen says sternly when I walk in. "The rabbi's on his way."

The rabbi's voice enters before he does. The voice

booms, "Who knows the story of King Solomon?" Then the rabbi marches in.

His bushy gray eyebrows jump into the air as he looks around the room. No one raises a hand.

"A long time ago in Israel, two mothers who had both given birth to sons came before King Solomon," explains the rabbi.

I wonder how old he is. He looks older than my parents but younger than Granny Fanny.

"The first mother said, 'This woman's son died when she slept on top of her baby and crushed him. She saw what she had done and took my son into her bed. Then she placed her dead son in my bed. I woke up and saw a dead baby boy next to me who was not my son.'

"The second mother replied, 'Liar! My son is the live one and your son is dead!' "

The rabbi points to Marci Gittenstein. "What would you do, young lady, if you were judge?"

She nervously shrugs her shoulders.

"King Solomon commanded, 'Bring me a sword! I will cut the baby in two.' "

Everyone in the room gasps! The rabbi raises his arms high over our heads until we're silent. He could be Moses standing on a mountaintop.

"The second mother said, 'Yes, divide the child, so he's neither hers nor mine.'"

"Ew!" cries David Hirsh.

"Quiet!" scolds Mrs. Cohen, tapping hard on David's desk.

The rabbi lifts his eyebrows again, smiles, and continues. "Hearing what's been said, the first mother turned to the king and said, 'Please don't kill the baby. I'd rather you give it to her.'

"That was all the king needed to hear. 'Give the first mother the living child, for she is his true mother!' he commanded.

"What do you think about this decision?" questions the rabbi. His eagle-eyed glance takes us in as he swoops around the room ready to gobble up the answer.

Danny Blum raises his hand.

"Yes, young man," says the rabbi.

"Only the true mother would want to prevent her baby from being cut in half, even if it meant giving the baby to her enemy."

"He was a wise king!" thunders the rabbi.

The story gets me thinking. My bossy arm again takes charge and shoots into the air. I try to yank it down, but not before the rabbi calls on me.

Rebecca is watching. She's wondering what I'm going to say.

"Rabbi, do you think twins are like a child divided in half?" I ask in a mouselike squeak.

The rabbi rushes over. "What an original question!" he says, his eyes burning bright.

I hear Rhonda and Susie giggling. The rabbi turns his head and they stop.

"Well," the rabbi continues, "I'm not sure what King Solomon would have said. But he would have made a multiple decision!" He leans back and roars with laughter. Our class laughs, too. He waves goodbye and walks out the door.

I like the rabbi. I wish he'd visit our class all the time.

The bell rings, and leaning in the doorway is a mysterious woman wearing dark green sunglasses and a pale green raincoat. She could star in the James Bond movie we just saw. A lime-colored scarf is tied around her hair.

It's Mom! But it's too early. Mom's always late.

"Come, twins," she purrs, and puts out her arms to gather us. Rhonda and Susie are gawking with wide-open mouths. For once, I'm glad Mom is Mom. I proudly swing my battered monkey and we leave temple far behind.

17

Monkey Land

It's my turn to choose what we'll do for our birthday with Dad, Mom, Granny Fanny, and Aunt Florence.

"I want to go to Monkey Land," I say for the hundredth time this morning to Rebecca. "It's my pick since you chose Parrot Rain Forest last year."

"Let's go to Parrot Rain Forest again," begs Rebecca.

We've been a zillion times. I know that bird show by heart. The white cockatoo rides the bicycle across the high wire and then the bright blue parrot shoots out of a cannon. Last year, six macaws were placed on our arms while

Dad took photos. One of the macaws pulled hairs out of my ears. I didn't know I had ear hair.

"Forget it," I say. "Miss Wilde showed me pictures of animals at temple for the Noah's ark bulletin board. One was an orangutan and I drew it. I want to see it in person."

"Just look in the mirror," says Rebecca in a creepy voice.

"If I look like an ape, so do you!" I snap.

"That's not nice, Rebecca!" says Dad. "It's Rachel's choice this year, and if she wants to go to Monkey Land, we are going to Monkey Land."

I can't believe Rebecca got into trouble. This is going to be a great birthday!

"Granny Fanny and Aunt Florence are here," says Mom, opening the front door.

"I hope they brought sweaters," mutters Rebecca.

I give her my best behave-yourself look.

"Happy birthday, twins," says sweet Granny Fanny. "I baked a coconut cake!"

"It's nice you baked a cake," says Mom.

Mom says this even though Granny Fanny always bakes us a birthday cake.

"It's nothing," says Granny Fanny. She brings it to the table, where forks, napkins, and plates are waiting. We all sit down.

We stare at the cake like island castaways who haven't eaten for weeks.

Mom slices everyone a piece while Dad pours milk.

Rebecca's and my plates are empty in seconds.

"Here are your gifts," says Granny Fanny, pulling packages out of her bag.

"Gifts! Schmifts! Wear them in good health," says Aunt Florence. She nervously fingers the green buttons on her frog-print dress.

Rebecca unwraps a blue woolly sweater and I unwrap a pink one. What a surprise. Not only does Granny Fanny always give us sweaters, she always gives a blue one to Rebecca and a pink one to me.

"I'll trade you my pink sweater for your blue," I whisper to Rebecca.

"Forget it," she says.

"Forget what?" yells Aunt Florence, pulling on the hem of her dress.

We shake our heads.

Mom hands us two fancy store-wrapped packages. We rip them open, and each of us finds a collection of plays by William Shakespeare. Rebecca gets *The Tragedies*. I get *The Comedies*.

"Aren't these too old for us?" I ask.

"It's time you read some real literature," says Dad, who never reads anything but the newspaper.

"I'm sure I can handle it," replies Rebecca.

"I'm sure you can, Miss Brainy-head," I want to say, but I keep it to myself.

"We're off to Monkey Land!" says Dad cheerfully. "Onward to the safari car!"

"Monkeys stink!" exclaims Aunt Florence when we are on the road. I can see from Mom's expression that she agrees.

"All God's creatures are good," says bitter Granny Fanny. "Be quiet."

Dad drives south on the highway for thirty minutes and turns at the huge MONKEY LAND sign. He parks under a gigantic banyan tree.

"What a beauty," says Mom. "I bet it's really old."

Long brown vines hang in strands from its big branches. Rebecca leaps over a long root.

"Come," says Dad. "I'm going to get tickets."

In the gift shop we go through turnstiles and enter the large caged-in walkway that winds through the park.

Spider monkeys are running over our heads and a few are hanging from the side. One with shiny eyes and a winning smile reaches toward us with a small dark hand.

"Get away!" cries Aunt Florence, leaning against Mom and almost knocking her down.

"Cut the drama!" yells Mom. "It can't hurt you."

Rebecca and I swing by a group of tourists masquerading as extras in a Tarzan film.

A man in a safari outfit and pith helmet empties a box of raisins into a metal cup hanging from a chain. The cup climbs through the air to the roof of the cage. It's lifted by two monkeys who quickly grab and eat the raisins.

"Aren't they adorable!" cries a lady dressed in a leopard print from head to toe.

Everyone snaps photos.

Something is falling on our heads. I look up and see a monkey dropping something.

"That might be monkey poop!" cries Mom.

"*Arrivederci*, baby!" yells Aunt Florence, yanking the belt on her skirt. "I'm out of here, pronto!"

"Please," I cry. "The monkey just dropped a raisin. I want to see the orangutans. I bet they're just ahead!"

We pass gorillas, chimpanzees, and then a sign pointing to an orangutan display.

"There they are," says Dad, smiling. "Big ugly apes with red hair. They have their own island."

A waterfall pours from a pipe in the side of the island

into a moat separating us from the monkeys. A large and a small orangutan sit on a branch of a fake-looking tree.

Orangutans are definitely funnier in person. I open my pad and start sketching the bigger one. I think it's watching Mom. Maybe it notices her because they both have red hair.

I shade the big gray pouches around its head with the side of my pencil.

Now the orangutan is lifting its arms toward Mom and I lower my sketchpad. The orangutan opens its mouth, throws back its head, and roars. It sounds more like a lion than an ape! The safari tourists arrive on the scene and snap more photographs. The watching crowd grows bigger and bigger as the orangutan continues to make a fuss.

The monkey keeper drops his broom and runs over to Mom. He cups his hand to the back of his ear.

"I can't believe what I'm hearing!" he cries. "This male orangutan is usually quiet and shy. That roaring noise is the orangutan long call! He's fallen in love with you, lady!"

"Keep that hairy monster away from me!" shouts Mom.

"An ape's in love with my wife?" exclaims Dad. "Enough monkey business! We're going home!"

We follow Dad as he walks quickly to the car. No one talks. I open my sketchbook and glance at my half-drawn orangutan. It's pretty good. I close it as Mom passes me her brush to comb the junk out of my hair.

Everyone in the car seems grossed out and mad. Except me. I'm exhilarated and trying not to laugh. I loved Monkey Land! Soon I can't hold it in. I start to giggle. Suddenly, Aunt Florence lets out a howl of laughter, then Granny Fanny joins in. Dad, Rebecca, and even Mom are close behind.

18

I Dream of Honey Cake

Our bus rolls in front of the school. I slowly climb down the black rubber-covered steps. I turn and see Rebecca's not with me. We left our house together but now she's disappeared. A redheaded patrol lady wearing Snow Orange lipstick blows her whistle and points for me to walk. She's holding a honey cake. Why is she holding a honey cake?

I walk into the school, past many closed doors. There must be a hundred! I turn a handle. It's locked.

"What are you doing here?" asks a man wearing thick Coke-bottle glasses.

"I'm looking for Mrs. Bunker's class," I say.

"You must be stupid if you can't find your class by now," he sneers. He's holding a honey cake, too. I hear children laughing behind the locked doors. I run out of the school.

"Where do you belong, young lady?" booms a female voice from high above.

I can't see her face. Her head must be in the clouds.

The bottom of an alligator-print skirt swings over green pointy shoes. A giant hand holds a honey cake under my nose.

"I'm lost," I explain.

"Lost! Lost! How can you be lost?" blasts the voice. The honey cake shakes in her hand.

"It's not my fault!" I cry. "I have only half a brain." I run away, and the black asphalt street rolls and twists under my feet. It throws me up high in the air. I'm falling! Below me is the university swimming pool, full of brown stuff. I wrap my arms around my knees into a cannonball and crash into something warm and sticky. Some of it gets into my mouth and I notice it's not too sweet. I can't lift my arms to swim. It's too thick and gooey. A big wooden spoon is stirring around me.

"Help!" I shout. "I'm sinking." Before I go under, I see a sign that reads TOP SECRET! KEEP OUT!! HONEY CAKE BATTER!!!

I rip my pink sheets off the bed and toss them to the floor. I sit up and hug Lion-o. Bright sunshine pours through our window.

"Rebecca!" I call out. "I had a scary dream. I got lost at school and creepy people were holding honey cakes. I couldn't find you and I drowned in honey cake batter!"

"Maybe you're hungry," she replies, lifting her head from her pillow.

"I hate honey cake!"

"You couldn't have a normal nightmare with monsters? No, Miss Original drowns in honey cake!"

"I got lost at school and . . ."

"Relax," says Rebecca. "Today's Sunday. We're not going to *school* school, but after Hebrew school we're going to Grandma and Grandpa's, who'll probably serve us honey cake."

After a busy morning and lunch, we pile into the car and drive to Grandma and Grandpa's. They are waving on the top steps. We troop inside and fall into the stinky chairs.

"Sit up straight, Rachel," commands Mom.

I sit up.

"Who's taller this birthday week?" says Grandpa, clapping his hands. He grabs our arms and helps us up. "Stand back-to-back."

Everyone watches.

"Look," he says, and again claps his hands. "They're just the same!"

We sit back down.

Grandma gets up and walks slowly into the kitchen. Here it comes. I lean forward in my chair and crane my neck to watch through the doorway.

As she cuts the red-and-white string and opens the cardboard box, I squirm in my seat . . . When she lifts it out and puts it on a plate, my feet start a tap dance on the carpet . . . Before she can cut the cake into four pieces, I jump up and dash into the kitchen.

"Who wants honey cake?" she asks.

"I don't," I whisper. I don't know if she's heard me. She blinks at me like a sad old robot in a daisy-print dress, then shuffles into the living room carrying two plates. Glumly, I follow her and take my seat. Only Rebecca seemed to notice my absence. She looks confused. Dad is telling Grandpa and Mom about the new line of shark-print beach towels he's carrying. Grandma is handing out the honey cake, one to Rebecca, one to me. I have no choice . . .

"No, thank you," I say. "I'm sorry, Grandma. I don't really like honey cake."

Grandma's eyes are hard to see because her thick glasses are smeared with something greasy. She's shaking her head, and I'm afraid she might start crying. Grandma takes my plate and slowly returns it to the kitchen.

"You don't have to eat it if you don't want it, Rachel," says Dad.

Grandma takes her seat.

"I'm proud you're thinking of your diet," says Mom.

"You snake," hisses Rebecca. "You get away with everything!"

That's it? All I have to say is I don't like it? No one cares except Grandma, and she doesn't seem to care now either. She's watching everyone else eat their cake but me.

Grandpa jumps up and claps his hands. "Anyone like a ginger ale? I know Rachel would!"

I smile as Grandpa hands me a frosty glass.

Grandpa watches me drink and asks, "What kind of cake do you like, Rachel?"

"Ice cream," I whisper.

Grandpa claps his hands and says, "We take turns. One week we eat ice-cream cake and one week we eat honey cake. How about that?"

I nod and smile.

Mom says, "Ice-cream cake sounds fattening."

"Not if it's once in a while," replies Grandpa, giving me a wink.

19

I'm an Artist

Our good thoughts are flying your way!

There's a pretty stranger in Mrs. Bunker's class today. She's wearing a short yellow shift, and her pale blond hair is teased into a tall beehive. There is a pencil sticking out of her hairdo. Recently, Blondie wore a new beehive-styled wig and explained it was the latest fashion.

"I'm Miss Ray," she says, and smiles. "I'm your substitute teacher. Mrs. Bunker took ill over the weekend."

Today I won't see a dying bird.

"What is the class working on?" Miss Ray asks.

No one raises his or her hand.

"I'll be here while your teacher's out," she says in a

voice that rings like a bell. "I have some math and science worksheets to keep you busy until I speak with her. I'm not grading them so just have fun."

I stare at the worksheet and walk to the back of the class to the encyclopedias. Pinky waves and follows me.

"Isn't it great Birdbrain's not here?" she says. "Maybe she just flew away."

I nod.

"Did your dad tell you he bought a ton of patchwork jackets from Grandfather's tribe?" she asks.

"No," I say. "But I love my jacket and wear it when I watch TV."

"Well, my grandfather thinks your dad's great," she says.

"Sit down, girls," says the musical-sounding Miss Ray. "Now get to work, everyone!"

"I better go back to my seat," says Pinky, hurrying off.

Because of Miss Wilde's encouragement at Hebrew school, I'm drawing animals from pictures instead of from my head. I grab the *A* encyclopedia and carry it to my seat. I turn to "Animals," and flip through page after page of animal pictures. The buffalo looks interesting. I pick up my pencil and sketch his big body. My buffalo fills the whole piece of notebook paper. I draw a lot of wavy lines for grass. At the bottom of the drawing I write "Buffalo."

I turn back a page and stop. There's an anteater. It's so different-looking from the other animals. I like its long nose and long bushy tail. I try to make my drawing look like the picture. I add a small bird on its bushy tail and write "Anteater and Friend" on the bottom of the page.

I'm starting an orangutan when Miss Ray walks by. I panic as she asks, "What are you doing?"

I hide my drawings with my hand and say nothing.

"Is that a drawing?" she asks.

I'm in trouble. I should be completing my worksheet. She's going to send me to the principal's office. Some kids never return from the principal's office.

"I see drawings," says Miss Ray. She gently pushes my arm out of the way and picks up my buffalo and anteater. I silently say goodbye to the class.

"These are wonderful!" she exclaims. "You're a budding little artist. I want you to work on these every day I'm here! Would you like to borrow this encyclopedia and take it home tonight? I want to see lots of drawings from you, young lady!"

Her soft brown eyes and sweet face remind me of Little Star, my guinea pig, but without his teeth. Or fur.

Miss Ray, can you be my teacher forever?

All week she's wonderful and I'm sad she'll be going. But on Friday afternoon, right after lunch, Miss Ray makes an announcement.

"As you can see, your teacher hasn't returned. I found out today that she'll be out a few more weeks. It's time we make get-well cards. I'm sure she'll enjoy our little rays of sunshine, and they'll help her get better faster."

I want her to get well, but not too fast.

"Making the cards will be today's art project. Later we can all vote on the nicest and most thoughtful card."

She hands us each a piece of paper and crayons.

I had another weird dream last night, but it wasn't scary like the honey cake nightmare.

All the dead birds Mrs. Bunker couldn't rescue came alive. They flew into her thick gray braids and made a giant nest. The birds chirped and sang songs. They laid one blue-and-pink-speckled egg. Twin birds hatched out. They fluttered off Mrs. Bunker's head and soared into the bright blue sky.

I write across the top of my paper "We are your baby birds." I draw a big nest filled with a cardinal, a blue jay, a mockingbird, and a few birds from Parrot Rain Forest. I put a book under one wing of every bird and a pencil under the

other. For my finishing touch I add a big smiling sun sending out rays from above. I write across the bottom "Our good thoughts are flying your way!"

Granny Fanny would be proud.

"It's time to finish," says Miss Ray at last. "And please don't forget to write your name on the bottom of your artwork. I am going to pick up your wonderful drawings and display them in front of the class. You can quietly come up and vote on the small pieces of paper on my desk."

No one speaks as they silently come up to the front in small groups and study the drawings. Simone looks pleased. And even the biggest jerks, Eddie and Tony, are quiet.

One at a time, we cast our votes.

"Now, study chapter five in your grammar books while I count your votes," she says.

I'm so excited I couldn't study even chapter five of *The Tree Boys*. I look at the same page of my textbook for what seems like forever. I won't look up at Miss Ray, for fear of jinxing myself.

"We have a winner!" Miss Ray exclaims, waving her pencil in the air. She tucks it into her beehive and smiles. "Rachel Ringwood is our favorite artist!"

ARTIST! Did I hear Miss Ray say I'm an artist?

Simone leans over and whispers, "Good going! I voted for you."

"Come up here, Rachel. I brought in a small prize," says Miss Ray. She hands me a clear plastic palm tree filled with colorful candy and gives me a hug.

"Thank you" is all I can utter. My face is as hot as a volcano. I keep my head down and carefully take my prize so no one can see tears erupting.

"All your cards and greetings will make Mrs. Bunker so happy!" exclaims Miss Ray as the bell rings.

I show my prize to Rebecca and Georgie on our bus ride home.

"That's really nice," says Georgie.

"Neat!" says Rebecca.

I can see Rebecca's really pleased. I can't wait to show my prize to Mom.

I have a new theory.

Rebecca and I share a room. We share our clothes. We share our friends. We share our looks, but we don't share our brain. Rebecca's brain is for schoolwork. My brain belongs to an artist.

The bus comes to our corner and we jump off. I run into the house, throw my books on the table, and cry, "Look, Mom! I won first prize for my artwork in school!"

"That's nice," she says unhappily. She looks at my prize and sees that the palm tree is filled with candy. She grabs it. "You know I don't allow candy in the house!"

Mom walks to the toilet.

"No, Mom!" I cry. "Please . . ."

She opens the palm tree and pours the candy into the toilet. She flushes it. I watch it go down, but some bubbles up and floats in the water. She flushes it again and hands me the empty palm tree.

All of Biscayne Bay drains out of my eyes.

"I'm late getting to the beauty parlor and grocery store. Do you want to come or stay home?" she asks.

I lift my head and see Rebecca standing in the doorway. She was watching the whole time! We shake our heads and say, "No, we want to stay."

We hear Mom roar away. Rebecca mumbles something about homework. I throw the empty palm tree into the trash. I've decided to really disappear. I walk into our closet and pull out my suitcase from the top shelf. I pack some clothes, grab Lion-o, and hurry out the front door. I make it to the last step and sit down. I need a plan. I hold Lion-o close and see that his left ear is about to come off. Lion-o looks lousy but he doesn't care. I don't care either.

I'm tired of hearing "Stand up straight!" "Why can't you

be beautiful like your mother!" "You eat too much!" "Go wash your ears!" "Why can't you be smart like your sister?" "Go take a shower!" "Why can't you learn math!" "Why can't you speak like a human being!" "Your breath stinks! Go brush your teeth!"

At the end of *The Tree Boys*, Kip, Tim, and Baby Bark's entire family moved out of the tree hut. Big Fangs, who could climb trees, was trying to eat them. They traveled until they found a steep cliff that was out of reach of tigers, lions, and leopards. Kip and Tim shouted for joy because they knew they were safe at last.

If the Tree Boys can leave home, so can I! Will anyone miss me?

I'm thirsty. I should run away after a quick glass of orange juice. Mosquitoes are buzzing my face. I hate mosquitoes. I should start walking before it gets dark.

A station wagon drives by slowly. I lean into the shadows so it doesn't see me. Lion-o's head feels damp from my drippy tears. The door to our house opens behind me and cool air sweeps over me. Rebecca steps out, shuts the door, and sits down.

"What are you doing?" she asks.

"What does it look like?" I snarl. "I'm running away from home."

"Where are you going?" she asks.

"I'm going to walk and walk until I get far away!" I answer.

"Please don't go," says Rebecca.

"Mom and Dad won't care if I'm gone," I sob.

"Yes, they will," says Rebecca.

"No, they won't!" I snap back.

"I'll miss you," she says.

"Why?" I ask. "All I do is mess things up. You're always mad at me."

"You know, Rachel," says Rebecca, rubbing her new nose, "you're not the only one who messes up. I do, too."

"You do?" I ask.

"Yes, I feel bad I blamed you for chasing me through the glass door. It wasn't your mistake. I hit you on the back and yelled, 'Tag, you're it!' Either one of us could have gone through the door. I didn't want to admit it was all my fault. I'm sorry."

It wasn't my fault? Rebecca forgives me?

"Rachel," continues Rebecca, "you're my best friend in the world, and I don't want to wake up tomorrow without you. Please come inside. Please don't leave me here alone."

She puts her hand on my arm and pulls me to my feet.

We walk into the house and she shuts the door. I follow her to our room. She pulls my suitcase from my hand, unpacks it, and puts everything away, including the suitcase. I place Lion-o under my pillow and see Rebecca's new blue sweater waiting there, too.

"Oh, I traded sweaters," she says. "I'm sick of blue."

"You are?" I ask.

"Not really," she replies.

"Thanks," I say.

"Let's go up on the roof," says Rebecca.

We haven't been up on the roof together for ages. I stop by the bathroom for a tissue and blow my nose. Then we go outside and climb the oak tree at the side of the house. It's an easy climb and the roof is only one story up. The sun is shining bright as we step out on the shingles.

We hear Blondie singing. We walk toward her voice and see she's hanging freshly washed sheets on the clothesline out back.

"Try me," she sings as she lifts a sheet to the line.

"Hi, Blondie!" we say.

Blondie looks around, surprised. "Where are you girls hiding?"

"Up here!" we answer.

She looks up and smiles. "Hello, Rachel! Hello, Rebecca! Now, children, you be careful if you're going to sit up there."

"Blondie, I won first prize for my artwork in school today!" I say.

"Why, that's wonderful, child! I'm tickled to my toes." She waves, picks up her empty basket, and continues singing back into the house.

I hear chattering and see squirrels chasing each other up the mango tree in our backyard. Cardinals are circling above the highest branches. A blue jay squawks and flies between them. They're saying, "We're alive, Mrs. Bunker, we're alive!"

"Wait here," I say to Rebecca. "I'll be right back."

I climb down the oak tree and run back inside the house and into the kitchen. I grab some green grapes, a few ice cubes, two plastic cups, and a bottle of orange juice. In the garage I find a basket and a rope. I climb back up to the roof with the rope tied to the basket handle, then I pull up the basket and bring our picnic to Rebecca.

"I'm proud you won the art prize today," says Rebecca.

"I've never won anything in my life," I blurt out.

"Rachel, you're going to be a great artist someday," she says. "I wish I had your imagination!"

"You do?" I ask.

She nods.

We sip our juice. I love the jingling sound of ice cubes. I imagine Kip, Tim, and Baby Bark climbing in their jungle home where there are no ice cubes. I'm not sure I could sleep in trees or swing naked from vines if there were no ice cubes. I guess maybe I don't want to live with the Tree Boys after all.

Rebecca and I sit quietly until Mom drives up and gets out of the car.

"We're up here, Mom!" yells Rebecca.

"Come help me with the groceries," she calls with a big smile. "I'm making Rachel's favorite dish for dinner tonight!"

It's Mom's way of saying she's sorry.

The sunlight sparkles off her freshly set hair and rhinestone sunglasses as she disappears into the house. Mom looks beautiful after her visit to the beauty parlor.

Dad will be home soon. And tonight we're eating burnt-skin chicken! I smile at Rebecca. She's smiling, too!

The palm trees in front of our house are bending and waving hello in the gentle breeze. Our hair blows softly around our faces. It isn't too hot and it isn't too cold. Everything feels just right.